Love Money and Murder

CLIFFORD C. LEARY

authorHOUSE®

AuthorHouse™
1663 Liberty Drive
Bloomington, IN 47403
www.authorhouse.com
Phone: 1 (800) 839-8640

Published by AuthorHouse 07/23/2015

ISBN: 978-1-5049-1750-6 (sc)
ISBN: 978-1-5049-1751-3 (e)

Library of Congress Control Number: 2015909458

Print information available on the last page.

Dedication

Rita Leary, my wife,
who provides constant support to my writing effort.

Donna Leary Mentzos, my daughter,
who assisted with the editing.

June M. Leary, my daughter,
who provided the encouragement, support and editing
without which this book would not have been written.

⇥ Preface ⇤

As I sit back in my rocking chair, sometimes with a glass of wine, many of the people, places and circumstances of my past go through my mind. I daydream of what was and wonder at what might have been.

I was born at the onset of the Great Depression and raised on a stony 200–acre dairy farm in central Wisconsin. Instilled with the belief that hard work and determination were the keys to success, I left home at seventeen and went to work with a construction company erecting silos.

When the construction season was over, I signed on as a station helper for the Soo Line Railroad. Over the course of the next four decades, I worked my way up through the ranks to Vice President of Transportation at Minneapolis, Minnesota.

I also married and raised a family of five children.

After my retirement, I returned to the place of my origin. I now share time with my 104-year-old mother and enjoy the closeness of my brothers and sisters.

Life was always interesting and sometimes exciting. At the age of eighty-four, I enjoy putting some of my thoughts on paper and hope you will enjoy them too.

Cliff Leary

⚔ Love, Money & Murder ⚔

BOB NASON SAT ON the old handmade lawn chair basking in the noon-day sun at the south side of the cabin. He and his father Will had just finished a fine lunch of fresh blue gills they had caught that morning. A slight zephyr out of the west moved the tops of the tall pines at the south end of the small clearing surrounding the cabin. Bob watched as a deer moved quietly through the undergrowth then stopped and eyed him suspiciously with its ears open full forward so the slightest sound could be heard. Bob's thoughts were of the many wonderful days he had enjoyed there. The fresh air and the serenity were captivating. In less than a week, Bob would be returning to join the Class of 1971 as senior at Highview High School in New Brighton, Minnesota.

Bob was tall for eighteen with blond hair and a winning smile. A good student, he was looking forward to the beginning of classes even though it meant there would be little time available to spend at the cabin.

The cabin located north of Hinkley, Minnesota had been built by Bob's grandfather in the 1940s. It was constructed mostly

1

of logs cut right from the surrounding forty acres of forest. In one end of the cabin was a large stone fireplace. The stones came from the site as well. The cabin had been a get-away for the family ever since. Although Grandfather Nason had been gone for several years the place was still called "Grandpa's cottage."

"Time to get to work son," said Will as he came out of the cabin carrying a small bag of fertilizer and a can of fuel oil. They were clearing stumps and old trees from around the cabin.

Boom, boom, crash! The sound of the blast reverberated through the forest. The ground shook as tree stumps and debris flew through the air. The acrid odor of the blasting mixture permeated the air and blue smoke rose with the flying debris.

"Stay back Bob; that big pine is still leaning," yelled Will. This was dangerous work so they had to be careful.

"Ya, I'm watching it," yelled Bob.

"Did you see the bear?" asked Will.

"No, what bear?"

"A big old sow and two cubs took off running down the logging road just before the blast."

"Maybe they had an idea what was going to happen."

"Could be. Well, son, bring the shovel and fertilizer and we will set up for another round. We will have to make about three more blasts before we bring the cat in to pile these stumps down at the other end of the field."

"OK, Dad. Looks like somebody is coming in the driveway."

"It's Pete the Game Warden," said Will. "I wonder what he wants?"

Pete parked his pickup truck and walked over to Will and Bob. "Hi guy's, what's going on?"

Will said, "Hi Pete, we are doing some clearing so we can put in a little garden."

"I see. Some of the people down in Hinkley could hear the blasting and wondered what was happening. Are you using dynamite?"

"No, just a little fertilizer and fuel oil. It packs enough power for this job."

"OK, men, don't get hurt." He went back to his truck and left.

"Why did he ask if we were using dynamite?" Bob asked his father.

"Well son, we might have required a permit if we were using dynamite."

"And we don't if we use fertilizer?"

"Right, at least not now. Not too many people know how to use it. Well, let's get on with it so we get done before somebody else complains."

They finished just as a neighbor, Hank Nelson, showed up with his caterpillar. He shoved the stumps into a pile at the far end of the opening and leveled out the field. It would be planted in corn and a few vegetables in the spring to provide food for the wildlife.

⚜ Back to School ⚜

THE BELL RANG. IT was the first day of the 1970-1971 school year at Highview High. A noisy group pushed and shoved their way into the crowded hallways. There were happy smiling faces as many of the students renewed their friendships with their classmates. Seniors Bob Nason and Johnny Edwards were among this group. They had shared several classes before and had played on the baseball team their junior year.

They had not seen much of each other during the summer so this was a welcome reunion.

As they checked their schedules, they found they would be in several classes together this semester. They both seemed pleased at the prospect. John was tall, dark and slim with a rather mischievous smile.

"What did you do all summer, Bob?" John asked.

"I spent quite a bit of time up at my grandpa's cabin. I did some fishing and water skiing. Had a good time actually. What did you do?"

"My grandpa has a farm in Wisconsin. He has more work than he can handle so I was sort of his hired hand for the summer. I helped with the cows, the haying and stuff like that. I didn't get paid a whole lot, but did manage to save up a few bucks."

"Gee, Johnny, that sounds like fun. Do you think you will want to become a farmer?"

"I don't think so, driving the tractor and some of that stuff was fun but I wasn't too keen about getting up so early in the morning and milking those darn cows."

"I can imagine. Say man, did you notice there were a few real hotties going into our first class?"

"No, I was too busy checking out the good looking teacher that just walked in. Get a load of that bright red hair and those big brown eyes. I bet she isn't over twenty- one years old."

"Oh oh, looks like you like them a little older, eh John?"

The first hour bell rang. Bob and John were in rapt attention.

"My name is Miss Swanson. I will be your English teacher this semester. You look like a great class and I am looking forward to teaching you many things you have no interest in knowing."

"Let's go around the room and have each of you introduce yourselves to me and the class."

Most in the room were acquainted with each other from prior years but there were several new students. Bob and Johnny took seats in the same row, with Bob in a seat directly behind Johnny. They each took particular note of the two new girls in the seats adjoining them. John turned for a quick look at Bob and rolled his eyes a little toward the new girls. Bob responded with a knowing smile. This could get to be a fun year.

The room took on a jovial mood as Miss Swanson continued with a get acquainted session asking students what they had done over the summer. Some had traveled, some had worked and some had been bored.

Soon there was roll call and then assignments. It was time to get on with the studies.

The bell rang and it was on to the next classroom.

Bob and John hung back a bit watching to see if the new girls were going to be in their next class as well. It turned out they were, so the boys followed closely behind and managed to again take seats beside the new girls.

"Hi! Well here we are again. My name is Bob Nason and this is John Edwards, usually called Johnny. And you are Shirley Nolan, right?"

"Yes, nice to meet you both and this is my friend, Betty Hanson."

"Hi guys, nice meeting you," said Shirley.

"Hi. You can call me John or Johnny, whatever. Nice meeting you. Where did you go to school last year?"

"We were both at Edina, but our families moved to New Brighton during the summer."

The teacher called the room to attention.

"All right, let's cut the chatter. My name is Mike Brown." He wrote his name on the blackboard.

"That will be Mr. Brown to you, thank you." All chuckled.

"I am also coaching boys basketball this year and we are in need of some new blood in that department so I would like to encourage you guys to come on out and join the team. And girls,

I understand we are short of cheerleaders and pom-pom girls so ladies lend a hand. Sign up and cheer our players on to become winners."

Mr. Brown picked up his roll call book.

"Okay, sound off as I read your name." He read each name from the book and they responded, "Here." After class, Mr. Brown called Johnny and Bob aside and pressed them further to consider basketball.

"You guys are both about six foot, look like you are in good shape and I'm sure would make a good addition to our team. Think about it." They both told him they would give it serious consideration.

And so it went throughout the day on the first day of school. The girls and boys were in several of the same classes and became better acquainted. At the end of the last class, they met in the hall.

Bob asked, "Where do you girls live?"

Betty, the tall blond, slim with a very pretty face and just a few freckles said, "I live down on the end of Pike Lake Road and Shirley lives two houses north. Where do you guys live?"

Bob said, "We both live on Highview Drive, that's not very far from where you live."

Johnny said, "Well, how about we walk home together?"

"Sounds okay with me," said Shirley who was a little shorter than Betty, had dark hair and slightly rounded cheeks. Her smile indicated a fun loving personality.

Bob piped up, "You know, I've been thinking Johnny, what do you think about signing up for basketball? Shirley and Betty would you consider signing up for cheerleading?"

"Wow, sounds like Mr. Brown really got to you," said Shirley.

"Well, I think it would be fun. I would kind of like to play and it would be great if you girls were there as cheerleaders."

Betty said, "I sort of like the idea but I want to talk it over with my mom first."

"Me too," said Shirley.

Johnny said, "Doggone, I'm game, let's do it."

They went down to the gymnasium, found Mr. Brown and got signed up. The girls accompanied them and Mr. Brown again urged them to sign up for cheerleading.

The four walked home in high spirits. They were all happy with their newfound friendships.

Shirley said, "Hi Mom, home from school. It was a great day. Betty and I got acquainted with some new friends."

"Male or female?"

"Male, Mom."

"Oh oh! Tell me all about it."

"Well, there are these two neat boys who sat right beside us in class and we found out they live right over on Highview Drive. They walked home with us and they are going to be playing basketball."

"Who are the boys?"

Mrs. Nolan was very interested. She wanted to find all about the boys her daughter was so enthralled with.

"One of the boys is Bob Nason. He is tall and blond. The other boy is Johnny Edwards. He is not quite as tall as Bob, but still quite tall. He has black wavy hair and I think brown eyes. They both seem very nice."

"Sounds like you had a very interesting first day at school. How do you like your teachers?"

"They are OK. Mr. Brown, the basketball coach, wants us to sign up to be cheerleaders. What do you think of that Mom?"

"Is that something you really want to do?"

"I guess I would like to. The boys said they would sign up for basketball if we girls would sign up for cheerleading or pom-pom."

"Is Betty going to?"

"She is going to ask her mom tonight. What do you think; is it okay Mom?"

"Sure, go ahead, just so it doesn't interfere with your studies."

"Thanks Mom. I will call Betty and tell her so her mom will know you said it was okay." Shirley dialed the telephone. "One - two - three- four— who's the team we're rooting for? Five - six - seven - eight - who do we appreciate? Highview High, rah-rah-rah."

"Hi Betty, I got an okay from Mom. Have you asked your mom yet?"

"No, I am going to wait until supper time when dad is here."

"Okay, be sure to let me know, talk to you later."

"Okay, bye."

The boys were walking along home after having left the girls off.

"Well, what do you think of those chicks, Johnny boy?"

"Not bad, not bad, Bobby. I think Betty Hanson must be Swedish with that long blond hair and blue eyes, and I bet Shirley Nolan is Irish with her long dark hair. Let's face it, they are both beautiful girls."

"Couldn't agree with you more and they both seem really nice."

"Yes, I hope they take up cheerleading and we get to play on the basketball team."

Bob arrived home and breezed through the front door.

"Hi Mom."

"Hi Bobby. I have a fresh batch of cookies in the kitchen. How was your first day at school?"

"Pretty good. Where are the cookies?" Bob shoved a warm chocolate chip cookie into his mouth.

"We met a couple of girls and walked them home."

"Who is the other half of we?"

"Oh, John Edwards. We were in some classes together last year. He lives right down the street on Highview. He has not been around all summer because he was helping on his Grandpa's farm over in Wisconsin. He is a nice kid. We are pretty good friends."

"OK. So tell me about the girls."

"They sat right next to us in a couple of classes so we got acquainted right away. They both live over on Pike Lake Road. They are Shirley Nolan and Betty Hanson."

"Oh I think I know their mothers from Spanish class at Moundsview Tech. What a coincidence. This is all so exciting. What else is new?"

Bob grabbed another cookie.

"Well, Mr. Brown is the basketball coach and he asked Johnny and me to go out for the team. What do you think?"

"You will have to talk to your dad about it but I think it will be okay. He played basketball when he was in high school."

Bob swallowed and grabbed a glass of milk.

"I hope it will be okay because we actually signed up this afternoon."

And so it was, the boys played basketball and the girls became cheerleaders. They became constant companions and the very best of friends. They were regulars at the school dances and attended the prom in the spring.

High School Prom

THE FOUR WERE QUITE popular at school. Wonder of wonders, Bob was elected prom king and Betty was chosen as queen.

This was the first real pairing of the two. Prior to this, the four were really just great friends. Although they spent a lot of time together, they had not really chosen partners. This event changed that.

The members of the promenade court were announced at a general assembly at school. There was clapping as each name was called and that individual went up on the stage. Shirley and John were named as members and then there was a standing ovation when Bob and Betty were announced as king and queen. The court then assembled on the stage as the entire student body clapped and cheered. It was a memorable day at Highview. It was an exciting walk that afternoon as the four made their way home.

The prom committee had much planning to do. They had to select a date, a location, a band, decorations and all the necessary details. The members of the court were fully engrossed in these preparations. Bob and Betty played a leading part in the planning.

Finally the big day arrived. The hall was filled with boys dressed in their finest and the girls all beautiful in their flowing formal gowns. There were cheers as the orchestra struck up the school song and the couples flowed out onto the floor.

"Oh Bob," exclaimed Betty as she threw her arms around his neck and hugged him, "Was this meant to be? I just couldn't be happier. You really are a king."

"And you, my dear, are definitely my queen."

They danced slowly around the floor, holding each other tenderly in the subdued light of the ballroom as the band played softly on into the night.

"Betty, I think we are becoming much more than just friends."

"Oh Bob, of course we are, I have loved you for a long time. It seemed you just didn't notice." She laid her head on his shoulder and kissed him on the neck. They danced over to the refreshments table, toasted each other and he kissed her full on the lips.

"Wow- this must be some punch," said the chaperone who was minding the bowl.

"Great stuff, we will each have another," said Bob as he held up his empty glass.

It was obvious that John and Shirley were also enjoying each other and dancing closer as the evening progressed. They changed partners occasionally but mostly remained together. There was of course a lot of cutting in by others wanting to dance with the king and queen. It was a wonderful evening. They were all having a great time.

Eventually the dance was over and it was time to leave. The boys opened the doors and helped the girls into the old Cadillac convertible Bob had borrowed from his father. The long gowns and beautiful girls demanded the utmost in chivalry on this occasion. They were thrilled to be using the car. It was a 1953 Cadillac Eldorado, glistening light sand color with white sidewall tires and lots of chrome.

Bob pulled the Caddy out of the parking lot and headed downtown for a late night snack at Shiek's restaurant. The car purred along quietly as the occupants cuddled, continuing to enjoy the fun filled evening.

As they proceeded down Central Avenue, they didn't notice a vehicle approaching from the west on Washington Avenue at a high rate of speed. The car failed to stop at the red light and crashed into the side of the Cadillac.

The girls screamed! The collision spun them around and shoved the tangled vehicles onto the curb. The interior of the Cadillac was littered with broken glass and the side was caved in almost to the center of the vehicle.

Betty was bleeding and crying in pain. Blood ran from a large gash on Bob's head. Shirley and John were pinned in the back, barely conscious.

The police arrived momentarily. They had been following the speeding car and its drunken driver. They called for two ambulances and wrecking equipment. Bob and Betty were taken to the hospital immediately as well as the intoxicated driver of the other car. It was necessary to use the jaws-of-life to cut down the side of the car to remove Shirley and John. They too were rushed to the hospital.

After the emergency room doctor finished treating him, Bob went to a pay phone in the hall. "Dad, I'm so sorry. I've got some real bad news."

"What is it? Are you Okay?"

"Oh Dad, the car got smashed. A drunk driver blindsided us and everyone's hurt." Bob's voice trailed off. He leaned against the wall, woozy.

We got blindsided at Central and Washington by a drunken driver. We are all at the emergency room at St. Mary's Hospital. We each have some injuries but I don't think any are real serious. Will you let the other parents know?"

"Don't worry, son. Just stay put. I'll call everyone and we'll be right down."

"Okay Dad, I love you."

"I love you too, son. Don't worry. It will all work out."

All the parents soon converged at the hospital, attempting to determine the extent of the children's injuries. It was soon found that Shirley and John had been severely shaken and bruised and experienced concussions but no broken bones. Betty had suffered a broken right arm, a fractured ankle, and multiple lacerations from the broken glass, including a deep gash in front of her right ear. The cut on Bob's head had stopped bleeding but the area was quite swollen. The doctors wanted to observe Shirley and John overnight for possible complications from their concussions.

Betty had to have her arm and ankle x-rayed and placed in casts. She was kept at the hospital for observation in the event of shock. Bob was permitted to go home with the understanding if the swelling increased or if he developed a severe headache, he was to return immediately.

The following morning Bob's father checked with the police department and found the Cadillac had been towed to a police storage lot. He also learned that the drunken driver did not have insurance and that the police would be pressing charges on multiple counts.

The loss of the Cadillac was a blow to Bob's father. He had inherited the car from his father. It had never been driven during the winter. It had been kept in the garage and covered most of the time. The wreckage had to be disposed of so Mr. Nason contacted an antique car dealer and sold the car to him for parts.

When the dealer picked up the car it was loaded on a truck and brought to the street in front of the Nason's house. The neighbors gathered to view the wreckage. They all knew the car well as Mr. Nason had frequently given the neighborhood kids rides on nice summer Sunday afternoons. Many took pictures and many cried at the sight of it. Even the Mayor and his wife showed up. They had ridden in the car many times at parades and other special events. The Mayor's wife hugged Mr. Nason and said, "It is so sad."

Mr. Nason had difficulty holding back the tears as he told them all it had been his parents' car and they had loved it too. The New Brighton newspaper carried an article about the history of the car and the sadness felt by the whole neighborhood when it was destroyed.

Despite her injuries, Betty was able to continue in school using a crutch. Bob's head healed quickly. However, they were all emotionally traumatized by the accident. The incident seemed to bring the four more closely together for the balance of the school year. It was a sad situation for the student body. The joy of the prom was dampened by having the king and queen injured in an auto accident.

Betty was left with a scar in front of her ear and an almost imperceptible limp as a result of her ankle injury. They would forever be a reminder to Bob of his love for her and the wonderful times they had enjoyed together.

When school was out they spent a lot of time together for the first week or two. Then Johnny left to help on his grandfather's farm. Shirley took a job at The Soo Line Railroad downtown and Bob took a part-time job with the Minneapolis City Engineers office. Betty started doing volunteer work at the hospital. They were all busy but they did get together on a few weekends during the summer. They were all trying to save their money and planned to attend the University of Minnesota in the fall.

⚔ Grandpa Edwards' Farm ⚔

JOHNNY MOWED ALONG THE far edge of the hayfield pulling a hay mower behind his grandfather's John Deere tractor. As he drove along near the fence line of the neighboring farm, along came a horse and rider trotting along in the pasture on the opposite side. He waved as he continued to mow. It was evident the rider was a woman. She trotted off toward a wooded area and then turned back. She rode up close to the fence just ahead of Johnny and stopped. He stopped the tractor and was amazed to see he knew the rider. It was that good looking teacher from Highview, Miss Swanson.

"I thought that was you Johnny," she said. "Will you be here for the rest of the summer?"

"Yes, pretty much. What a surprise to see you. Do you live out here?'

"Well, I will be living here until school starts. The place belongs to my aunt and uncle but they have taken a trip to Europe this summer. I am staying here to keep an eye on the place. They are retired, have not been doing much farming but do have a couple riding horses that need to be fed and watered. If you would like to ride, stop over and we will saddle up the other horse."

"Sure, that sounds great. I will come over one of these evenings after chores."

"I will look forward to it. Nice to see you again Johnny." She turned the horse and headed away. Johnny recalled how attractive she appeared the first day he saw her back at Highview. Now, as then, she was a picture to behold. She sat high in the saddle. Her western style hat hung at the end of her long red tresses and glowed in the noonday sun. Something stirred inside Johnny as she turned, smiled and waved as she rode away.

It *was* hard for Johnny to concentrate on the mowing as he guided the John Deere round and round the hayfield. He kept thinking, *Man, she's some babe. I'm going to get over there and check out that other horse-- soon!*

There was still more hay to cut when Johnny went in to supper, so his grandfather asked him if he would continue mowing instead of helping with the evening chores.

"This is good drying weather, so if you get it all mowed tonight, it will wilt and then dry enough so we can rake it tomorrow and then bale the next day."

"That suits me fine Gramps. I guess you know I'd rather drive the tractor than milk the cows anyway."

"I sort of figured that, John. By the way, while you are out there, you might keep your eye out for a young gal on horseback. Old George and Emma Swanson are off on a trip and they have a niece looking after the place. She's a mighty nice looking young gal if I do say so myself. I hear she is a school teacher in town. You needn't mention this to your Grandma."

Mabel Edwards called from the kitchen, "What was that? You boys talking about me behind my back?"

"Oh no, Mable. I was just telling the boy here that you make the best pie a'goin."

"Yes, Grams, your pies are the best."

"Well, I'll see if we can whomp up a strawberry-rhubarb one tomorrow for you hard workers."

"And Ed, don't you be setting up our boy here with that red-haired siren across the back fence."

"Why Mable, how can you say that about a fine upstanding young niece of the Swanson's. And I understand she is a mighty fine school teacher too."

"Well, I don't know. Some of the ladies at church think she is overly attracted to boys."

Johnny piped up, "Well, this all sounds very interesting. I will let you know if I see her."

Johnny returned to the field and finished the mowing just before dark. It had been a long day's work. He showered and went to bed early.

Up early the next morning, Johnny helped Ed with the chores and gassed up the John Deere. By then Grandma had a big breakfast of bacon and eggs for her boys. They finished breakfast and went out to get things ready for raking hay.

It was a beautiful summer morning with the sun rising high and a light breeze from the west. The hay would dry fast. They hooked the John Deere onto the hay rake and pulled it out of the machine shed. Ed got out the grease gun and handed it to Johnny.

"Here you are lad; grease her up good. Look for all the grease fittings and pump the handle until you see grease moving out of the bearings. I'll check your work when you finish."

"Okay Gramps. We'll see how well a city kid can handle this job."

Under Ed's watchful eye, the grease job was performed well.

Next came the hay baler and it wasn't long before the machinery was ready to go to work. Johnny was a fast learner and a great help to his grandfather.

"Okay Johnny, let's take this baler out to the field and check on the hay. I know it is a little too early to bale but we will have the equipment ready. You take the John Deere and the baler and I will take the Farmall with the side delivery hay rake. We will leave the machinery at the opening in the woods at the end of the lane, right at the edge of the field."

"Okay Gramps. Let's get the show on the road." John hooked onto the baler and headed up the lane toward the field. Ed took the hay rake and followed. It was perfect hay drying weather. Ed wanted to take advantage of the weather and get the hay in without it getting rained on. They took the machines up to the woods and parked them in the opening.

"Well lad, let's check out the hay." They walked out into the field of new mown hay. The smell of alfalfa and clover permeated the air. It was a wonderful deep penetrating smell. A few grasshoppers jumped up in front of them as they walked in the field. Ed reached down and took a big handful, twisting and rolling the hay in his hands. He walked ahead and repeated the test.

"Well lad, it is not dry enough to rake yet. We will leave it until late this afternoon or evening and check it out again. If it dries today, we can rake it in the morning and start baling tomorrow afternoon."

"You mean you have to wait for Mother Nature Gramps?"

"That's right. We don't want to end up with moldy hay."

"So what do we do now?"

"Well, Johnny, we always have things to do around the farm but I tell you what, we have been working pretty hard, what do you say we sort of take the rest of the day off and rest up? We will probably have a long day tomorrow."

"Sounds good to me."

They left the machines and walked back toward the house.

"It is a little early but maybe Mable might be able to treat us to a cup of coffee and a piece of pie. How does that strike you lad?"

"Sounds like a winner. Say Gramps, as long as we won't be working would it be alright with you if I took the old pickup and went in to town for a bit? I'll see if anything is going on and maybe grab a cone at the Dairy Queen."

"Not a problem Johnny. Go ahead. Just try and be back in time for chores this evening."

They went into the house and Mable dished out a midmorning treat of apple pie and coffee.

"Thanks much, Gram. Great pie." He ate quickly as if he had something pressing on his mind.

"What's the rush Johnny? Have another piece if you like. I have another whole pie in the pantry."

"Gosh, no thanks, Gram. The pie is great but one piece is more than enough."

"Johnny is going to take the pickup and check things out in town. Sort of see what is going on and maybe he will see someone he knows. We can't rake the hay yet. I want it to dry the rest of the day so he is off duty until chore time and I plan to make use of the old hammock in the orchard."

"Oh, so I'm the only one who has to work today, huh? As they say, a woman's work is never done."

Johnny cleaned up, combed his hair, took the keys and headed out in the pickup. He did indeed have something on his mind.

Johnny drove down the road to the first corner, turned left and found what he was looking for. The mailbox read: Swanson, Box 222. He turned into the drive which circled around the house.

As he reached the back of the house his attention was called to the white boards of the corral and the two horses on the other side of the fence. He stopped near the fence, got out and the two horses trotted over to him. One was a pretty roan and the other was a calico. They each whinnied as he stood near the fence looking at them.

He noticed a covered barrel near the fence. He opened the cover. As he suspected, the barrel contained oats. He reached in, grabbed two handfuls of oats and held them out to the horses. They each went for the oats immediately. His hands tickled as the horses' noses worked his palms to get every kernel.

"Hey, what's going on over there?"

Johnny looked to his right across the back yard. Somewhat protected from view by a large lilac bush was a woman sunbathing. She was lying on a chaise in a very scanty sun suit. She was too far away for him to see clearly but as he expected, it was Miss Swanson.

"Hi Johnny, what's up? Come on over and sit a while."

"Hi, Miss Swanson. We are taking the rest of the day off to let the hay dry so I thought I would stop over and see your horses."

"Oh, well I see you are getting acquainted with them already."

"Ya, they sure know what is in the barrel."

"So I saw. They are both great animals and easy riders."

"So how are you doing Miss Swanson?"

"Johnny, we are not in school now so let's cut out a little of the formality. My name is Beverly so why don't you just call me Bev."

"Okay thanks Bev. I like that."

This seemed to drop any reserve he had been experiencing. As she was talking he couldn't keep his eyes off her. Her skimpy halter barely covered the nipples on her buxom bosom. Her flowing red hair hung over her shoulders and onto the back of the chaise. The red and white short-shorts barely covered the essentials. Her soft white skin was as yet not tanned. Her red toenails peeked out the end of her tiny straw sandals. This was real beauty lying here before him as he sat in the lawn chair beside her. He was embarrassed to look, yet he couldn't resist it. She had a tall drink on the lawn table beside her and a wide brimmed straw hat there too. What a picture, thought Johnny.

Bev smiled to herself as she watched Johnny taking her in. She was well aware of her effect on this young man. She had an inkling of his feelings even back in her classroom at school. There was somehow a connection, a vibe, an inner feeling that connected the two and it was somehow coming more to the surface at the moment.

"Would you like a glass of lemonade Johnny? I have a large pitcher in the fridge."

"That would be great, if you don't mind."

"Okay, I'll be right back."

Johnny watched as she arose, put her hand up over her head and smoothed out her red tresses, tugged her shorts down and adjusted her halter. She took her glass and headed for the house. Johnny swallowed hard. He couldn't believe what he was seeing. Her backside waddled just a little as she walked to the house. He wondered, was this natural or was it intentional for his benefit? At any rate he was definitely becoming more stimulated by the minute. Bev returned with a tall cool glass of lemonade in each hand.

"So Johnny, what have you been doing all summer?"

"Well, I have spent most of the summer thus far helping my granddad with his farming. It is a little too much for him to handle alone and hired help is hard to find. We are trying to get the hay put up right now and then we want to get at cultivating the corn so we will be busy for a while."

"Looks like you will be nice and tan and all muscled up before the summer is over."

"Ya, I suspect so. I do like the outside work but not too keen on the milking and stuff. What are you going to be doing all summer?"

"Well, like I said, I am babysitting the horses and watching the house so this is sort of a vacation. Although I am doing some studying, working on a masters."

"That is some nice looking horseflesh out there. Do you get to ride a lot?"

"Not a lot, but they do need exercise so I take one or the other out for a ride around the farm nearly every day. Would you like to do a little riding today?"

"I have never been on a horse in my life. I would probably fall off."

"Oh, I'm sure that wouldn't be a problem. I can give you a few pointers if you like."

"Well, why not. I can't stay too long though. I have to be back in time to help with the chores."

"Oh, we can be back in less than an hour. I will go in and put on some riding pants. I would get a little saddle sore if I went riding in these shorts. It will just take a few minutes."

She went into the house and returned with riding pants and a shirt. They went out to the corral and then to the barn. The horses followed looking for a handout of oats or a lump of sugar. Bev gave the bay a sugar lump and slipped a bridle on her, tossed the reins over a post and got a blanket and saddle from the rack. Johnny watched as she expertly saddled the mare. Next she gave

Calico a lump of sugar and slipped a bridle on him. Johnny stood nearby and then picked up the blanket and saddle and placed it on the gelding.

"Very good," she said.

Then they both bent over to reach under the horse for the girth at the same time. Their heads were close together and then their cheeks rubbed. Johnny pulled his head back as a feeling of warmth shivered through him. She turned her head and held a smile as her big brown eyes gazed at his for a long instant. Nothing was said but it was evident a message was being passed. They walked the horses out of the corral and into the field behind.

"Okay big guy, here is your steed. You take Calico and I will ride the mare."

She took his left hand and put it on the saddle horn then held the stirrup for him to put his foot into it.

"Okay, up you go." She gave him a friendly pat on the rump as he swung up onto the horse.

He took the reins, she mounted the mare and they were off. The horses started to trot and she told him how to rock in the saddle to smooth out the ride. It wasn't long before he had the hang of it and was enjoying the ride.

It was quite warm so they returned after a half hour or so. Now understanding the procedure, Johnny unsaddled both horses and removed the bridles as Bev watched.

"Well, you catch on fast."

"That was fun. Thanks for the lesson. I enjoyed it."

"Glad you did; you are welcome."

"Say Bev, it is still early, how would you like to go over the Dairy Queen for an ice cream?"

"Are you buying? If you have time, I do."

"Yes, I'm buying and we do have time."

They got in the pickup and were off. After a dish of ice cream and chit chat it was not long before their relationship became more and more friendly. They were enjoying each other's company a great deal. It was soon time for Johnny to start back so he dropped her off and headed for home for supper and chores.

At the supper table Grandpa asked Johnny about his day.

"Well, how was the trip to town, lad?"

"Well, Gramps, it was great although I made a little side trip."

"Oh, how's that?"

Fibbing a little about the detail, Johnny said, "Well, I went down to the corner and headed toward town but about a half mile past the corner, getting mail from the Swanson mailbox was Miss Swanson, my English teacher from high school. I stopped and chatted with her for a bit. She invited me in to see the horses and the first thing you know we took them out for a ride. Then later we went over to the Dairy Queen for a dish of ice cream."

"I heard that," said Grams. "You seemed a tad anxious to leave this morning. You weren't planning to meet that red-head all along were you?"

"Well, you heard Gramps mention about a nice young lady over there. I'll admit I was just a bit curious."

"Oh my! What will my friend Carla say when she hears about you meeting up with the red-head?"

"Now Mable, don't get upset. I have talked to her over the fence and she is a nice young lady. After all, Johnny had her in class all last school year."

"Well, I just don't know. Carla said a friend of hers had quite a bit to say about that girl. According to Carla's friend, that redhead has had quite a bit to do with quite a few young fellows."

"She is well-liked at school, Gram."

"Now Mable, I'm sure it will be just fine. Time to get those chores done lad."

Mable grumbled a bit under her breath. Ed and Johnny went out to the barn and got started with the evening chores.

The next day was beautiful. The hay was dry so Ed and Johnny were busy with raking and baling. Summer's work on the farm was well under way.

The summer passed quickly. Ed and Johnny were busy with the harvest, fence mending and care of the animals. There wasn't much spare time but Johnny did find a way to spend a little time with Bev. They got together for horseback riding, a movie, ice cream and conversation about once a week. They enjoyed each other's company and were becoming quite close.

On the last such evening at the end of summer before returning to the Twin Cities, they saw a romantic movie and returned to the Swanson's house.

"Would you like to come in for a bit Johnny? I baked a cherry pie today and there is ice cream in the fridge."

"Sure, it's still early and cherry pie sounds great."

They went in for the pie and Bev said, "These cherries are off the tree in the back yard. My aunt cans some for pie and my uncle makes a little cherry wine from the rest."

"Homemade cherry wine, huh? I bet that's good stuff."

"Sure is. Would you like to try a glass?"

"Why not?"

They each had a couple glasses of the smooth sweet wine and started feeling just a little bit giddy.

"Did I ever show you the house, Johnny?"

"No, as a matter of fact. This is the first time I have been inside. It looks like a very nice house."

"Well, why don't I give you the grand tour? Here, I will fill up your glass before we go."

They started in the kitchen. "These cabinets were made with lumber from oak trees cut in the woods out back. Some of the furniture in the living room was also handmade from the same lumber, as well as the bed and dressers in the main bedroom. There is some fancy carving on the headboards. Come on I'll show you."

They went to the bedroom and viewed the furniture and headboards. The wine was affecting both of them.

"I think I will just sit here on the edge of the bed for a minute," said Johnny.

"Oh oh! The wine is getting to you, eh?" She sat down beside him and put her arm around him.

"Well, it couldn't get to a nicer guy." She took his glass, placed both glasses on the dresser, returned and sat up close with her arm around him.

"You're not feeling sick, are you?"

"No, just a teeny bit light headed for a second there. I'm okay now."

"Here, I'll take your shoes off. You just lie back and rest awhile and you will be fine."

She took his shoes off. He laid back and she snuggled beside him. It didn't take long before nature took over. They were naked under the covers.

"I have never done this before, Bev."

"Don't worry. I'm a natural teacher."

It was almost midnight and Johnny realized he better head for home. This had been an experience he would never forget. They kissed goodnight and planed to meet again at her apartment back in the Twin Cities.

⚜ Students Again ⚜

S UMMER WAS OVER AND it was back to school. Bev had returned to her apartment and was teaching English at Highview.

The gang of four were all happy to be together again as they prepared to begin their university educations. Bob would be studying engineering. John would be majoring in Geology. Betty enrolled in liberal arts and Shirley selected English.

Summer was over but the warmth of fall still provided time for water skiing on Pike Lake, boating on the Mississippi, picnics on the sandbar and spending time at the Nason cottage up north. Life was good.

Frequent newspaper articles concerning expansion of the sewer system made them aware there were a number of caves under the city. Quite by accident they made a little discovery of their own. One day after a picnic lunch on a sandbar, they headed upriver toward the locks in downtown Minneapolis. As they neared the downtown area there was a small grove of trees and considerable underbrush overhanging the water's edge. They drove the run-about into the grove of trees and stopped to watch as barges were brought down through the locks. The fast moving current shoved their boat deeper into the trees and brush and to their surprise they soon saw what appeared to be a small cave in the limestone riverbank. Johnny separated some of the brush and pulled the front of the boat tight up to the bank. He stood up and peered into the opening.

"It looks like this hole opens up into a good sized cavern just a few feet in."

"Is it large enough to crawl into?" asked Bob.

"WOOOOH- that sounds scary," screeched Betty.

Johnny said, "Hold the boat still and I will see if I can climb partway in and get a better look."

He climbed up and into the entrance and was surprised at the size of the cavern.

"Hey, this place is big. There's plenty of room to stand up and it seems to go a long ways back. We have to get some lights and check this place out."

"Come on back down and hold the boat. I want a look at this too." Bob exclaimed.

Johnny got back into the boat, changed places with Bob and Bob went up into the entrance of the cave. He, too, was impressed with their find.

In the grove of trees and surrounding brush, the spot was quite well hidden. Their boat was completely hidden from outside view.

Johnny piped up, "Hey this is a wonderful secret hiding place. Let's keep this to ourselves and see what we can find out about these caves."

The girls were not all that interested but agreed they might go into the cave if it was well lighted. The boys discussed flashlights, gas lanterns and other possible forms of lighting they could come up with. They backed the boat out of the brush and into the river and headed for the boat landing. As they passed the sandbar they encountered a group of about fifteen young boys mooning them as they went by. The girls feigned embarrassment as they looked away and laughed. Bob hooted the air horn as he and Johnny waved.

That evening they went for a ride on the riverboat Jonathon Paddleford and danced as the on-board band played lively tunes. It was great to be together again.

Johnny and Bob went to the city library to research caves under the city. They found various newspaper articles which indicated there were indeed a number of caves under parts of the city but not much information on specific locations or size of the caverns. Nonetheless, their interest continued as they read articles on spelunking and the equipment used exploring caves in general.

A few days later, the boys returned to the secret spot armed with hammers, stone drills and a few other tools. They attached heavy metal hooks to the sandstone wall to which the boat could be tied and held securely. They also fashioned a step to provide easy entry from the boat to the cave.

They took flashlights and a gas lantern and entered the cave for a look around. The cavern was quite large. It was about fifty feet deep, forty feet wide and twenty feet high. A part of the ceiling was darkened indicating there had been a fire inside at some time in the past. A few pieces of charred wood and an ash pit provided further evidence that it had been a campsite.

"Could this have been an Indian camp?" asked Bob.

"Or a gangster hideout?" queried Johnny.

"Could be. There is certainly a story here at any rate." responded Bob.

The next weekend they planned a picnic in the cave. The girls were not anxious about it but the boys did a good sales job. They brought a small camp stove, two lanterns, a tarp and the makings for a cook-out. The tarp was spread out and four small folding chairs made the campsite complete. The girls were impressed as the boys prepared a tasty lunch. A portable radio provided music as they enjoyed the afternoon singing along and dancing.

The cave became a great hangout which they visited from time to time.

School was going well. Bob and Betty were going steady. Johnny and Shirley were getting serious. They were even thinking about becoming engaged.

⇥ The Call ⇤

ONE EVENING IN LATE fall, Johnny received a call from Bev. She wanted him to come to her apartment to discuss something. He went over and got the shock of his life.

"Johnny, I am pregnant."

"What?" You can't be serious."

"Yes, I can't believe it myself, but I missed my period so I took the test and it came out positive. I'm so shook up I can't think."

Johnny turned pale and started to perspire. "Is it possible the test could be wrong?"

"Well there is always a possibility but those tests are pretty accurate and besides I have been feeling a little crappy in the mornings."

Johnny looked at her and she didn't look so pretty now. Her hair was a little disheveled. She looked a little drawn and it appeared she had been crying.

"Holy shit, what are we going to do? I guess the first thing is find out for sure. There are several abortion clinics here in the cities. I understand all you have to do is stop in, they give you a pregnancy test and if you test positive they take care of the abortion and you are on your way."

"Well, I doubt if it is that simple and I'm sure it costs a bundle. Besides, I don't know if I want to have an abortion. That is taking a life you know."

"Bev, if you elect not to abort, you are going to ruin both of our lives. I am in no position to pay for raising a child at this stage of my life and how would you handle it as a single mother. Bev, just get the abortion and be done with it!"

"What about the cost? Do you have the money to pay for it? With my rent, car payment and credit card bills I'm broke. I'm sure they will want the money in advance. It will probably be a thousand dollars."

"Well, Bev, you just make the arrangements and I will see if I can scrounge up the money. Check it out tomorrow and we will talk as soon as you have the information. Okay?"

"Well, okay, let me know as soon as you have the money."

⤞ Deer Hunt ⤝

I T WAS A DRY and brown November. John was studying when the phone rang.

"Hi John, this is Bob. How are you doing?"

"So-so. What's up?"

"A couple of us are going to our cottage this weekend for a little deer hunting. How about coming along?"

"Gee, I don't know. I hadn't thought about going hunting this year."

"Well, you still have your rifle and stuff don't you?"

"Oh sure. I would just have to buy a license. What's the plan?"

"We will leave about six o'clock Friday afternoon. I will take our van and one of the other guys is taking his car and trailer and hauling a four-wheeler up there. We will come back Sunday afternoon. Not a big hunt but it will be a chance to get out in the woods."

"Okay, Bob. I will go along. I can stand a little change of pace."

"Good, have your stuff ready and we will pick you up around six."

Johnny was quite occupied with his personal problems but kept his thoughts to himself. The group met at the cottage for a break on Sunday afternoon. They wanted to make at least one more try for a big buck. Bob came up with a plan.

"Johnny, how about if you take the four-wheeler and ride straight south along the east side of the big woods. There is sort of a trail there. Go south until you come to a small opening and the trail will turn west. Go west about a quarter mile to an old logging road. This will take you right to the middle of the woods. It might take a while because the going might be a little tough in places. Circle back and make a little noise. You can toot the horn once in a while and even shoot a time or two. This should drive the deer north toward us. I will have the rest of the gang on deer trails up here. You should scare the deer up toward us and some of us will get some shooting. I know darn well there are a couple big old bucks that hang out down there in the middle of the woods."

"Sounds like a plan to me," said Johnny.

They all agreed it was a good plan and no one would have to do a lot of walking.

⚔ The Robbery ⚔

"OKAY, I'M ON MY way." Johnny went out to the four-wheeler. He hung his rifle on the machine, checked his holster for his pistol, checked the gas and started south.

He just couldn't get his mind off his problem with Bev and the need for the money for the abortion. *Damn it all, why the hell did she have to get pregnant? Where the hell am I going to get the $1,000.00? What if my folks found out? What if Shirley found out? What if she decided to keep the baby?* His mind was swimming and his guts were churning. He couldn't think clearly at all. He bounced along on the four-wheeler trying to collect his thoughts.

Up ahead he noticed the highway curved in toward the edge of the woods and down the road a ways he saw a Hinkley Oasis gas station. The back of the station was quite near the edge of the woods. He eased off on the throttle as he neared the station and noted there were no cars around. There was a large garbage dumpster in back of the station and he pulled up behind it. He stopped and sat there for a few minutes. Then, half crying he thought, *to hell with it!* He got off the four-wheeler, laid his rifle on the rack, and removed his orange hunting jacket so his back tag would not be visible. He had on an orange sweat shirt and orange pants. He pulled on his orange knit storm mask and darted to the store.

There was no one around outside so he ran inside. He grabbed a plastic bag from the dispenser near the banana bin, turned to the cashier, pulled out his pistol, handed her the bag and told her to fill it up. Startled and scared, she emptied the cash drawer into the bag and handed it to him.

"Now give me the bag from the freezer," he ordered. He knew some places kept the excess cash in money bags in their freezer. She hesitated.

"Hurry up." He pointed the gun at her. She got the bag and handed it to him.

"Now get down on the floor and stay there," he told her. She quickly complied and he ran out to the four-wheeler and took off down the trail.

He stopped when he reached the opening where the trail turned west. He put on his hunting coat, removed the mask and put on his hunting cap, stuffed the mask and bags of money into the big back pocket of his hunting coat and continued on. Dressed as he was in all blaze orange hunting clothes he knew he looked like all the other hunters stopping at the station so the cashier would have difficulty identifying him.

As he turned north to start the deer drive he heard a police siren off in the distance. Perspiring profusely, perplexed and confused, questions started racing through his mind. *Holy Christ, what have I done? Am I going to get away with this? What a dumb stunt! Should I turn myself in? Can I stay cool and get away with this? I just have to. We will be going home in the morning and I will be out of the area and safe.*

He continued up the trail on the four- wheeler, sounded the horn from time to time and shot into the air a couple of times. Returning to the others, he found that no deer had come through.

The hunt was over. They packed up their gear and headed for home. When they pulled out onto the highway Bob said, "I guess I better fill the gas tank. I don't think I have enough to make it back to the cities. I will just pull in here to the Hinkley Oasis gas station."

Johnny was perspiring nervously and said, "Okay, I'll do the pumping."

He noted the gas tank was on the side of the vehicle opposite the store so he would be shielded from sight while pumping. Bob went inside to pay for the gas.

When he returned he said, "Can you believe it Johnny, this place was robbed today. Somebody in hunting clothes came in, held up the place and disappeared. The police are inside."

"Well, for God's sake. Do they have a description of the guy?"

"Sort of. He didn't have a hunting coat on but had an orange sweat shirt and pants and left a particular kind of boot print on the floor."

"Did he get much money?"

"Sarah, the clerk, didn't say. She was pretty shook up by the whole ordeal."

As soon as Bob dropped Johnny off at home, he went to his bedroom to change out of his hunting clothes. He locked the door and counted the stolen money. It came to twelve hundred and fifty five dollars. It was certainly not enough to warrant the chance he took of getting caught and going to jail. It should be enough to cover the abortion, however.

Johnny didn't sleep all night. He got up early and went to a restaurant for coffee and a donut. He picked up a paper and there it was in the state news.

Duluth News Tribune
Sunday, Nov. 14 –Hinkley

Hinckley Oasis Station Robbed by Lone Gunman

Police are investigating the Sunday afternoon robbery of the Hinkley Oasis gas station. A masked gunman dressed in blaze orange and wearing a blaze orange mask entered the store and held up the clerk at gunpoint, escaping with an undetermined amount of cash. He left on foot and disappeared immediately. State police are investigating.

At seven thirty Johnny went to Bev's apartment. "Did you go to the abortion clinic?"

"No, I was waiting for you to come up with the money."

"Well, I went to the bank and got some of the tuition money I earned working for Grandpa last summer. Here is a thousand dollars. I am sure it will be much less than that. I called one place myself and they told me it wouldn't be more than seven hundred. Go get it taken care of. Call school and lay off sick and get it done today."

"Look who is telling me what to do with my own body."

"It is a simple matter for you to take care of it now. If you don't, you will screw up both of our lives."

"Okay, I will do it but if I have any problems later on you are going to pay and pay good. Do you understand that?"

"Okay Okay, don't worry, it will be fine."

Johnny went to Bev's apartment that evening. "So, how did it go?"

"Well, I drove over to the Meadowbrook Women's Clinic on Eighth Sreet South and it was pretty damn unpleasant, if you want to know the truth. I still feel pretty lousy. I'm not sure it was the right thing to do. I don't feel too good about it."

"I'm sure you will feel better tomorrow. What did they charge you?"

"They charged me eight fifty but I am keeping the rest for pain and suffering."

"Bev, that is not fair, but if that is the way you feel about it, keep the damn money."

"Well, damn-it Johnny it was your fault and now I have to suffer for it."

"Hey, wait a minute. You are the one that got me sloshed on wine and climbed into bed with me."

"Oh bullshit, you're the one that planted the seed."

"Well, that's water over the dam now."

Johnny left and felt that would be the last he would hear about her pregnancy.

In the following weeks, Johnny felt relieved and was more able to concentrate on his studies. He found his geology classes very interesting and he studied diligently. He also had a great deal of interest in what lay underground, under the city of Minneapolis. He gathered more information on the caverns and underground waterways.

Up early one morning, he grabbed a newspaper and coffee trying to catch up on the news before his morning class. An item in the Minneapolis Star Tribune caught his eye.

St. Paul Pioneer Press
Hinkley - Dec.2

New Evidence in Gas Station Case.

The State Crime Lab reports that following an investigation of the robbery of the Oasis Station at Hinkley, they have developed evidence which will no doubt prove to be very valuable in solving the case of the holdup on November 14th. A search is currently underway for a person of interest.

Johnny read it again and couldn't believe what he was seeing. He wondered what in the world they could have found. He decided he would just have to lay low and see what developed. This could become very serious.

⚔ Exploration ⚔

JOHNNY'S INTEREST IN THE underground caves and waterways deepened. He developed drawings of what existed. The central part of the city was built above caverns, tunnels and waterways. Some were natural and some were man-made.

The city library contained many articles relating to the exploration of the natural caves and the construction of underground tunnels for a variety of purposes. There had been consideration to use part as bomb shelters during World War II. There was ongoing concern about the danger of constructing large buildings above these areas. When caves were found under the existing Farmers and Mechanics Bank building, pillars were added underground to assure there was sufficient support.

A study made by a small group of young guys who called themselves "The Action Squad" provided a great deal of information they developed in their clandestine searching of most of the caves and tunnels in the Twin Cities area. Johnny was intrigued by their findings.

⇻ The Move ⇺

ONE EVENING JOHNNY'S PARENTS informed him that his father's job was being eliminated. His father would have to move to Chicago in order to remain employed by the same company. The family decided that it would be best for Johnny to stay in Minneapolis and continue his studies at the university.

Johnny found an apartment in the area near the grain elevators and the old Milwaukee Road railway station. It was not a very desirable neighborhood, but was close to downtown and the bus service to the university. It was also quite cheap which was important at the time.

His parents' move cost quite a bit. They took a loss on their house and would not be able to help with his tuition. Money was tight.

Johnny had a big surprise one evening when Bev called.

"Hi Johnny, how is it going?"

"Things could be better."

"Yah, things are not going too well for me either. I have been having big bouts of depression ever since the abortion. I have been seeing a shrink and he is pretty expensive. Johnny you are going to have to help me out with more money."

"What the hell? What are you depressed about? You would really have problems if you had not had the abortion."

"I know, but Dr. Malcom says this happens often. He calls it something like post partum something or other. Johnny, I need five hundred dollars bad."

"Damn-it, Bev, I think you've been playing me for a sucker. We only had sex once and that was in mid-August. You told me you missed your period toward the end of October. If you had gotten pregnant because we had sex in August, you would have known right away in September. It looks to me, babe, like you were screwing somebody else long after August."

"Why, you son-of- a-bitch! You are full of crap. You are the bastard that got me pregnant and that's all there is to it."

"Tell you what, girlie, you go back to the abortion clinic and get me your record. I'm sure they gave you an exam before the abortion so they could tell how far along you were at the time. Give me that record and we will see what it says. You are not getting another dime out of me until I see that record."

"Baloney, you come up with the money or there will be hell to pay."

"Good-bye, Bev!"

Pressure for money was beginning to weigh heavily on Johnny's mind. He worried about how he would handle it. He worried about his parents and how they were going to handle their situation and wished there was a way he could help them out.

As he studied the configuration of the caves under the city he noted there were voids under some of the banks. He read where The Action Squad had actually found a way into the sub-basement of the Soo Line building. It was right next to the First National Bank. He thought about the possibility of getting to the vault of the bank through the caves.

⇥ Research ⇤

THE POSSIBILITY OF SOLVING all his money problems by robbing a bank kept recurring frequently. As he studied the location and size of the caverns in the downtown area, it seemed to be more and more realistic that it would be possible to break into a bank vault from underground. There was a large cavern under the Farmers and Mechanics Bank but the location of the vault in the bank was not located immediately above the cavern. The Federal Reserve Bank seemed to be out of the question inasmuch as the caves did not extend that far north. He recalled that the Action Squad had been able to enter the sub-basement of the Soo Line building by following narrow caves in that area. The Soo Line building was right next door to the First National Bank so this seemed to present the best choice for further investigation.

As a geology student, he became friendly with some of the men in the city engineering and structures department. They were helpful in providing him with information about the underground sewers and tunnels as well as the soil and rock types. They also permitted him access to a variety of surveying and measuring devices which could determine the precise location of the vault from underground.

John visited the bank and rented a safe deposit box. The safe deposit area was actually a part of the vault but separated from the money storage area by a gate made of metal bars. Large trays of bills were plainly visible through the gate. While pretending to add items to his safe deposit box, he used his small camera to quickly photograph the entire vault area.

He noted the vault was an old one, almost ten feet square. The huge iron door was stamped, Diebold Safe and Lock 1871. It had a card attached to the inside indicating it had been inspected in the 1910's and 1920's.

The next day he returned with a small laser level and laser ruler in his pocket and determined the distance and direction from his lock box to the exterior walls of the main vault. Using an altimeter he determined the height above sea level of the vault floor. Further checks in the ensuing days enabled him to precisely locate the vault. He prepared a drawing and added the various measurements.

Now to find this location underground. His study determined that from the location of his apartment near the grain elevators, it was only a short distance to the opening of a huge storm sewer that emptied into the Mississippi River. There was water in the storm sewer only after heavy rains or snow melt. It was designed to drain storm water from the downtown area. He was able to walk into the storm sewer and find a location near the bank.

Returning to his apartment and studying the cave formations, he was able to determine there was a cave extending from beneath the bank right up to the storm sewer. By removing some of the bricks from the wall of the sewer he would be able to enter the cave and get right under the bank.

During the next week, as time permitted, he worked at removing brick from the sewer wall. The wall was more than a foot thick but by chipping away with a hammer and chisel he was able to work his way through.

The cave extended as far as he could see in the direction of the bank. The cave was only about four feet, floor to ceiling, so he could not stand up but could easily go through on hands and knees. The floor of the cave seemed to be soft sand but the ceiling was a hard smooth rock.

Johnny went to the city library to see what he could find about soil underlying the city. To his surprise, there was an abundance of information. He found that the topmost layer under the city was called Platteville Limestone. Under that was a layer of Ordovician Shale, a hard smooth layer and below that was a material called friable St. Peter Sandstone.

With access to the building permits being issued at the city engineering office he soon determined most of the buildings had their footings on the layer of Ordovcian Shale.

After making the hole in the wall of the storm sewer he was able to enter the cave and crawl toward the bank and get right under the vault. Above his head he saw the hard layer of Ordovcian Shale. He took out his altimeter and took a reading. Referring to his notes it appeared the layer of shale was about eighteen inches thick.

In order to double check the location of the vault, Johnny took the steel head of a nine-pound maul to the bank and placed it in his safe deposit box. Later he returned to the cave with a pinpoint metal detector. The detector was able to detect the location of the maul. Johnny marked the spot. By measuring from that point he was able to locate the center of the vault above him.

His spare time the next couple of days was spent at the library searching for information on the construction of old Diebold vaults. He wanted to obtain as much information as possible to determine the most vulnerable location to enter the vault.

His search indicated it was likely the sides and top were solid concrete about sixteen inches thick in which were embedded steel bars both horizontally and vertically. Then three quarter inch steel plate on each side of the concrete. This would be tough to get through. The floor however was most likely simply about six inches of concrete poured right on top of the shale. This would mean it would be necessary to go through the eighteen inches of shale and then six inches of concrete to get into the vault from the bottom.

Johnny sat back in his old easy chair pondering the best way to proceed. He wondered if he should really go ahead with this dastardly deed. He wondered if he could really pull it off. He wondered about the best way to cut through the rock and the bottom of the vault.

⚜ Shooting Practice ⚜

JOHNNY'S PHONE RANG. "HELLO."

"Hey, how have you been? I haven't heard from you in ages."

"Hi Bob. Oh, just been busy with the usual stuff, you know, school and a part- time job.

"Well, are you busy this weekend? I am going up to the cabin Saturday and coming back Sunday. How about coming along and we can get caught up. Maybe wet a line or shoot a few clay pigeons."

"I do have things to do but, darn-it, I could stand a day off. Sure, I'll go, when are you leaving?"

"How about I pick you up about nine thirty Saturday morning."

"Great, see you then."

They stopped at Toby's restaurant at Hinkley for coffee and a cinnamon roll and arrived at the cottage well before noon.

Bob said, "Tell you what Johnny, I'll warm up a few hot dogs, and then we can reload some shotgun shells and see what kind of a shot you are."

"You mean you reload your own shells?"

"Oh sure, it's much cheaper than buying new ones and reloading is kind of fun. If you want a little extra bang, you can use a little extra powder."

"That sounds interesting. You will have to show me how to do it."

"Not a problem."

They had a few hot dogs and soda for lunch and got started on the reloading.

"Bob, where do you get the supplies, the powder and stuff?"

"Oh most gun shops stock it. I have been getting it at Guns-N-Stuff. It is a sporting goods outfit over near Crazy Louie's on Washington Avenue in St. Paul."

"This powder must be a little dangerous to handle."

"Not really. Just don't get it near too much heat or a sharp shock. There is a list of caution stuff on the container."

Bob brought out a cardboard box filled with empty shells, a box of primers and a container of gunpowder. He showed Johnny how to reload the shells. John was quite interested in the process. They prepared a couple dozen shells and went out back to a clay pigeon thrower.

The clay pigeons could be thrown safely up into the air over a deep ravine and wooded hillside. They took turns shooting and operating the thrower. Bob was quite an expert as he had done this many times. Johnny did surprisingly well for a beginner, however it didn't take too long for him to develop a sore shoulder from the kick of the twelve gauge shotgun. As he looked over the area he noted a pile of tree stumps at the end of a small field.

"What is the deal with the stumps and the field, Bob?"

"Well, that area was once covered with a stand of big white pine trees. A few years ago, we cut off the trees and sold the logs to a sawmill, then we blew out the stumps, worked it up and planted some corn. The deer fed on the corn and when hunting season opened we usually had a buck or two hanging around. We didn't manage to get the corn planted the last couple of years."

"How in the world did you blow all those stumps? It must have taken a lot of dynamite."

"We didn't use dynamite, we used fertilizer."

"Fertilizer?"

"It is really simple. You mix ammonium nitrate fertilizer with a little fuel oil and whammo, you have a bomb. Would you like to see how it is done? I think we still have a bag or two of fertilizer left over from fertilizing the corn."

"Yeah, sure. Bring on the fireworks. Fourth of July coming up."

They went into the cabin and in a tool closet beside the big stone fireplace they got a bag of fertilizer and everything necessary to make a small explosive device. Bob went through the details step by step as Johnny watched intently. Bob looked in the kitchen wastebasket and found an empty bean can. He prepared a length of fuse and filled the bean can about half full of the prepared mixture.

"Okay Johnny, bring these matches."

They went out to the stump pile, placed the can under a big stump at the farthest edge of the pile, and stretched the fuse out on the ground.

"Okay Johnny, light the end of the string and run like hell up the hill."

They ran toward the cabin and waited. They could see the small flame following the fuse toward the bean can. In a short while it reached the can and --- Booooom! That big stump went flying into the air with a dozen pieces shattering in all directions.

"Holy Moses, Bob, I can't believe the power in that small amount of fertilizer. Where in the world did you learn about that stuff?"

"From my Dad. He used to work for a demolition company. Remember the old Dykeman Hotel downtown? He helped implode it. He did a lot of other demo work around the state. He learned about explosives when he was in the army. The trick is figuring out what size explosion you want and then preparing the appropriate size charge."

"Wow, I am impressed. I sure learned something today. Thanks, Bobby, old boy."

"Not a problem. Well my friend, I think it's about time we start thinking about a little supper. How would you go for some pizza and beer?"

"Sounds good to me. Do you have pizza here?"

"No, but I'll have some brought out."

Bob got on the phone and called the Hinkley Oasis station.

"Hi, may I speak to Sarah please? ----- Hi good looking. How are you doing? ---- What time are you getting off work? ----- Five o'clock? Okay. What are you doing after work? ----- I see. ---- Is Mary there too? ---- Uhhuh.----- Well listen, I am up here at the cabin and I have a friend from town with me. How about bringing up about four medium pizzas and a couple of six packs of Bud and have supper with us? Oh, and bring a jug of Jack Daniels and some Squirt too, Okay? ----- I will pay you when you get here and maybe add a special little tip. Thanks, sweetie. See you."

"Okay Johnny, we will have beer, pizza, booze and company. How does that grab you?"

"Sounds good to me. These girls work at the Hinkley Oasis station?"

Johnny sat back in his chair and felt his face getting flush. *Oh my god, I hope this is not going to be the girl I held up at the station. Could she possibly recognize me? God, I can't believe she could. I was completely covered except for my eyes.*

"Are you feeling alright Johnny? You look a little red in the face."

"I'm okay. My stomach is just a bit growly."

"How about a little antacid? I have some Tums right here in the cupboard."

"Sure, maybe that will do the trick, I will take a couple."

Johnny took a half dozen Tums and said his stomach felt better.

The girls arrived about five thirty. Bob met them at the door and helped bring in the supplies. Johnny stood back a bit to get a good look at the girls. They came in laughing and joking with Bob. Johnny recognized Sarah as the girl he held up but said nothing. Bob made introductions all around. There was no indication from Sarah that she recognized Johnny.

"Well, let's get these pizzas in the oven and pop open a couple of Bud's. Johnny if you will serve the beer I will get the oven started. There are glasses in the cupboard."

Johnny got glasses and poured beer for all four. He kept a sharp eye on Sarah but there was no hint of recognition. It wasn't long until they were all chattering away enjoying the beer and pizza.

The conversation died down a little after supper so Bob said, "How would you like to hear some great music? You won't believe it but I have an eight track player and a bunch of really good tapes. They haven't been played for a while. Let's limber them up a bit."

Bob got the tape player working and started playing some great old big band dance music. He turned up the volume and grabbed Mary for a spin around the room. Sarah looked at Johnny and said, "Hey, they are pretty smooth. How about giving them a little competition?"

"Well, I'm game if you are."

He took her hand and they waltzed out onto the floor. Johnny was a good dancer. After a couple of waltzes they were all warmed up and needed to rest a bit. Bob opened up the bottle of Jack Daniels and mixed a drink for each of them.

Mary said, "Wow this is turning into a real party."

Sarah said, "And how! Just what we needed after a hard day's work."

"Speaking of work, tomorrow is Sunday, do you ladies have to work tomorrow?" asked Bob.

"Nope we have the day off for a change," said Sarah.

"Great, how about staying over and making a night of it? There is plenty of room."

"Probably not a good idea," said Mary.

"We will think about it," said Sarah.

"Okay, let's drink to that," said Bob and he poured another round of Jack Daniels.

More music, more dancing and more booze. It was a great party. Johnny and Sarah got cozy and ended up in a bunk at one end of the cabin and Bob and Mary took the bunk in the loft.

Johnny awoke early and lay there thinking, *Geez, I can't believe I would end up in bed with a gal I held up. I sure wish that had never happened. It was all because of that damn Bev.*

It wasn't long until Bob was making noise at the stove and the smell of bacon and eggs filled the room.

"Come and get it!"

They all enjoyed a hearty breakfast as the bright light of the morning sun filled the room. The girls sat across the table from the guys.

"Wow, this place looks different in the light of day," said Mary.

"And you guys are much better looking in the daylight," piped up Sarah.

Mary said, "Hey Johnny, your eyes are two different colors. One looks hazel and the other looks brown."

"That is right. My eye doctor says it is quite common among guys with a little French blood in their heritage. It indicates they are great lovers. It is said some men can change the color at will and in the process hypnotize the girl in their arms."

"Really, I'll be watching out for you buster," said Sarah. They all had a good laugh.

"So, I understand you guys both went to Highview High together," said Sarah.

"Yes. We have been friends for a long time. We both played basketball and a few other sports," said Bob.

Mary said, "I have a cousin that went there for a couple of years. She used to tell about a couple of hot blooded teachers."

"Oh, who were they?" asked Bob.

"I don't remember the names and I don't know if it was really true or if it was just a wild rumor, but she said she heard one of them would have sex with a guy, then later claim she was pregnant and blackmail him for money. It sounded pretty wicked to me."

"Wow, I guess. I wonder who that could have been?" said Bob.

Johnny lost his appetite.

After a long breakfast and more chit chat it was time for the girls to leave and time for Bob and Johnny to head back to the Cities.

❧ Bev Calls ❧

WHEN HE ARRIVED HOME, Johnny's answering machine light was blinking. He played the message.

"Hey Johnny, this is Bev. I am getting sick of waiting for you to pay up. I am hurting and I need money for the shrink and I need it now. I need a thousand dollars and I need it by ten o'clock Monday morning. You better get it over here or I will have to talk to somebody about a little caper at a station at Hinkley. Call me!"

What the hell could that bitch know?

Johnny was thoroughly ticked off. If she did know something about Hinkley it would be very bad indeed. Johnny thought about it for at least a half hour. *"Enough is enough"* he muttered aloud to himself.

Johnny went over to the Ace hardware and bought a bag of lawn fertilizer and some lamp oil. He returned home and prepared an explosive using a plastic milk bottle. He placed a cap on the bottle. He then took a plastic aspirin bottle, filled it with gasoline, capped it and taped it to the milk bottle.

After dark he went over to Bev's apartment building. He stayed in the shadows, found her car and secured the bottle to the exhaust pipe of her car, adjacent to the muffler.

There won't be much left of that bitch when that little poultice warms up. That should be the end of my trouble with her.

He slunk away, hurried on home and poured himself a stiff drink of whiskey.

A Bottle of Wine

Bev called JR liquor. "Is Benny there?"

Benny was one of the partners. He took care of all the deliveries and pretty much handled the finances. Benny was a rather small mousy fellow with a receding hairline.

"Hi Benny, I really need your help again. I have been so depressed and I am way behind in my payments to Dr. Malcolm. Could you fix me up with another thousand right away?"

"My God, Bev; you are milking me dry. What the hell does that shrink charge you anyway?"

"I know it's a lot, but, honey, you do like me to be in a good mood when you come over don't you? And of course I have to be very careful that I don't accidently say anything to your wife, Sherri, when I see her, don't I?"

"Okay, okay, I'll see what I can do."

"Oh, sweetie, could you bring along a bottle of cream sherry when you come?"

Gruffly he said, "Okay, but it is going to be late. I won't be able to come until after closing and I have a couple other deliveries to make."

"Well, love, I am tired and feeling so down, I might be in bed when you get here. I will leave the door unlocked so you can just leave the bottle on the kitchen cupboard and leave the money in the cookie jar."

"Okay, bye."

Benny was burning inside. *That damn blackmailing bitch has got to be stopped. Who the hell does she think she is? I should never have gotten tangled up with the likes of her.*

Benny found a bottle of cream sherry, carefully cut the seal, poured out a couple ounces and dropped in a half dozen dark black capsules. He then carefully resealed the bottle.

After closing the store, he made a couple of deliveries and drove over to Bev's apartment. The door was unlocked so he went in quietly, left the bottle on the cupboard and cash under some cookies in the jar before he left. If his plan worked out he should be able to find a way to retrieve the cash.

⚜ Buick for Bev ⚜

B EV CALLED WALTERS BUICK at Rosedale and asked for Don.
"Hello, this is Don.

"Hi Don, are you on a private line?"

"Yes, I am in my office on my private phone, what's up?"

"Well, Donny, I guess it is about time to make the deal on that red convertible; my car doesn't want to start. The battery seems to be dead."

"I see, well, why I don't pick you up. We can come back here and take care of the paper work and then I will send someone to tow your car in. The convertible is ready to go so you could drive it home."

"Okay, now let's go over the deal once more so we are in agreement on everything."

"Sure, no problem. I will give you the car for wholesale plus five percent and allow you five thousand for your car."

"Oh, I thought we talked about wholesale less six thousand for my car when you were here last night."

"Well, sweetie, I think the boss would fire me if I write up a deal that good."

"Well, Donny, we wouldn't want your wife to find out about our little ah - relationship now would we?"

"Geez, Bev, you wouldn't blackmail me right out of a job would you?"

"Let's not call it blackmail, Donny. Let's just call it a favor for a favor. You have been enjoying our time together haven't you?"

"Well, of course, but I thought you were, too. I didn't realize our relationship was a business transaction."

"Don, you are a big boy. You know a girl has got to do what a girl has to do."

"How about that blue 2008 sedan? Maybe I could give you a sweet deal on it."

"No, I have my heart set on the '09 red convertible. Could we save your butt if we just cut out the plus 5 percent and I give you straight wholesale and you allow me six grand for my car?"

"Bev, you are killing me. The only thing I can do is pay the five percent out of my pocket. It would have to come out of our savings account and I don't know how I can do that without my wife finding out about it."

"I guess you will just have to invent a little story, Don. Can you pick me up this afternoon? I might even have a little candy for you if you come alone."

"Okay, I'll be there about two o'clock."

Damn! I should murder that bitch! How did she ever rope me into this situation?

Don became more and more upset. His blood was practically boiling. He was a big guy, six foot four, two hundred fifty pounds of solid muscle. He sold cars and was a professional wrestler on the side. His dark complexioned face turned red. He got up out of his chair, slammed the office door and charged out, walking around the car lot.

With his blood pressure at the bursting point, Don left about one forty five and drove over to Bev's apartment. He parked several spaces away from her car and went up the stairs to her door. She met him at the door dressed in a red satin housecoat having a large rope sash around her waist. Without a word from either of them she took him by the hand and led him directly to her bedroom.

The minute they were inside the bedroom he threw her on the bed. With a beet red face, glaring eyes and perspiration streaming down the sides of his face, he throttled her, pressing hard on her neck as she squirmed and kicked trying to escape his grasp. He did not let up. Unrelenting and with his knee on her stomach, he continued until her face turned blue and there was no life left in her. All the while he had been swearing and calling her every name he could think of.

He turned her lifeless body over on its back and, holding the shoulders down, he grabbed her hair and snapped her head back with a powerful jerk breaking her neck. He removed the rope from around her waist, tossed one end over the door and tied it to the knob on the other side. He placed a chair in front of the door. With his strong arms he raised the body up and tied the rope around her neck leaving her feet dangling a few inches above the floor. He tipped the chair on its side. The scene now looked like she had hung herself. He swore at her and walked out.

As he walked through the kitchen he noticed a bottle of wine on the cupboard.

"Damn, just what I need," He mumbled to himself. He took the bottle and hurried out to his car. He opened the bottle, took two big drinks, started his car and headed for the garage. After only a few minutes his stomach felt upset, his vision became distorted and he became sleepy. *"What the hell is in that booze?* He reached for the bottle to look at the label and took a smell. He spilled some on the seat and floor.

"Damn strange smelling hooch," he mumbled to himself as he dropped the bottle.

He was driving about seventy- five miles per hour when he went completely blind and crashed into a concrete bridge. His car flew into the air, rolled over several times and rolled down the embankment. The police arrived and found him dead at the scene.

Johnny read the morning newspapers and noted the following article with interest. He had watched Bulldog in wrestling matches a number of times.

Minneapolis Star and Tribune

Wrestler Dies in Car Crash

Prominent wrestler, Don (The Bulldog) Rust, was killed in single car accident on I-35 yesterday afternoon. Police are investigating. Alcohol is suspected.

Johnny really opened his eyes when he saw the following article in the St. Paul paper. He could not believe she would have committed suicide. This was strange indeed.

St. Paul Pioneer Press
New Brighton

Local Teacher Found Dead

Highview High school teacher, Beverly Swanson, was found dead in her apartment. Friends say she had been suffering from depression. Suicide suspected.

The next article really got his attention.

St. Paul Pioneer Press

Unexplained explosion at the vehicle holding yard.

The car owned by deceased school teacher, Beverly Swanson, was taken to the Maryland Avenue vehicle holding yard awaiting final disposition. It was parked along the chain-link fence adjacent to the railroad tracks. For as yet unknown reasons, it burst into flame. It was destroyed along with several adjacent cars. A small grass fire, which was believed started by a spark from a locomotive, is suspected to have reached the area and ignited the gas tank of the car.

Johnny read the news several times, and then sat back for another cup of coffee. *"Well that is not the way I had it planned but I guess that ends the blackmailing"* he muttered to himself.

⚜ Bank Job for Betty ⚜

"HI, BOB, GOOD NEWS. I just got the job at the bank. What say we go out tonight and celebrate? I have been saving up. I'll buy dinner at Murray's."

"Wow Betty, you must be in the bucks. Dinner at Murray's isn't cheap."

"Well, I did get a little money for my birthday so I can handle it."

"Okay, big spender, I will pick you up at seven o'clock. Oh, does that include martinis?"

"Yes, but only one. That's all you can handle."

"Ha, ha. See you at seven."

Bob picked Betty up at her home and they drove downtown to Murray's.

"Well, Bob, we haven't been out to dinner in quite a while. It is some state of affairs when I have to call you up for a date. What is the matter, Bob, is the old ardor cooling off? Do I have to start looking over some of the other boys around here?"

"No, no, Betty. Don't do that. It's just that I have been pretty busy with homework and my part-time job. I have to work as much as I can or I will not be able to afford the tuition and expenses; but let's make it a point of getting together more often."

"Do you ever see Johnny? I haven't seen him for a coon's age," asked Betty.

"Not much. I try and touch base once in a while. We did get together for a couple of days during deer hunting but that's about it."

"So, Betty, tell me about your new job at the bank."

"As you know I had a little part-time job at Target but it was only a couple hours a week so I put my name in for more hours at the First National Bank and finally they called me."

"Will you be working a lot of hours?"

"Not really, but it works out well with my class schedule. I will work afternoon's from one until five and on Saturdays, one until closing at three o'clock."

"Not bad. Do you know what you will be doing?"

"Well, I understand I will be handling the lock box area and watching the vault."

"Geez, you will be right next to the big money right off the bat."

"You know me, honest face."

"Well, Betty, I am going to be one of your customers. I have been thinking of getting a safe deposit box for some of my – ahem - valuable stuff."

"I start next Monday, so I'll be looking for you."

They had an after dinner drink and called it a night.

Several weeks later----

Minneapolis Star and Tribune
Another station robbed.

The Oasis store at Eau Claire, Wisconsin was robbed at gunpoint last evening. A man wearing an orange ski mask and orange hunting clothes held up the store. It appears he left on foot running into the wooded area behind the store. Authorities arrived within minutes, locked the doors and gathered evidence. The store was re-opened for business within an hour.

And a few days after that:

Minneapolis Star and Tribune
Oasis at Chippewa Falls robbed.

At about 10:30 p.m. last evening, the gas station at Chippewa Falls, Wisconsin was robbed at gunpoint. It is assumed the robber was the same as the one who held up a similar station at Eau Claire earlier this week. The robberies are similar to the one that occurred at Hinkley, Minnesota last fall. Hinkley Oasis management advises they will be offering a substantial reward for the apprehension of this thief.

⤞ Girl Time ⤝

"HI SHIRLEY, I HAVE news. I just got a job at the First National Bank. With you at the Soo Line, we will be working real close together."

"Oh, that's great. When do you start? We can get together for lunch."

"I will start on Monday and I will be working from one until five so if I come in at noon we can go to lunch and both go to work at one o'clock."

"Great, let's meet in the Soo Line lobby at noon and have lunch at the Nankin."

"See you there. This will be fun. Bye, Shirl."

This was the first of many noon-hour get-togethers between the two friends. Shirley worked full time in the accounting department at the Soo Line and Betty part-time at First National while she attended college part-time.

In reviewing some of the accounts at the Soo Line, Shirley found that the Soo furnished steam for heating the First National Bank building. It was necessary for her to go to the sub-basement of the Soo Line building from time to time to review old records stored there.

One day to satisfy her curiosity, she went into the boiler room and noticed a tunnel with a large steam line leading from the Soo Line building to the First National Bank. The tunnel was not large, but she was able to go through and found herself in the sub-basement of the First National with a stairway leading to the basement of the bank. From the basement, a stairway went up to the lobby. She returned to the Soo Line building and under her breath said, "I guess I had better keep this information to myself."

Betty was enjoying her new job taking care of the safe deposit boxes and records of people who came and went, placing or removing items from their boxes. On days when she worked until bank closing, she assisted in locking the big door to the vault.

Betty was quite mechanically minded and the locking mechanism intrigued her. It was old, having been installed when the bank was built many years ago, and the clock, gears and levers that all worked together were interesting. One day when no one was around, she took several pictures of the mechanism. She perfected her drawings until she knew exactly how everything functioned. The timer was set so the door could be unlocked in the morning when the bank opened for business. The timer mechanism had to be in the proper position to allow the combination lock dial to turn and release the lock. Through careful study she was able to determine how the timer released and what the combination numbers were. *She would be able to open the vault! Wow, I better keep that information to myself!* This was scary. If the bank was robbed she could be blamed.

One afternoon Shirley showed up at the bank at five o'clock.

"Hi Betty, how about going down to the Radisson for a drink?"

"Okay, I will just lock up my record book, close the vault and we can go."

Betty did not have a class that day, so off they went to the Red Room for drinks. They each had a couple of manhattans and decided to stay for dinner. Talking over old times was fun.

As they got up to leave the bar to go to the dining room, Betty asked, "What happened to your coat Shirl? You have a big stain all across the side?"

"What! I never noticed. I must have rubbed up against something dirty without knowing it."

"Oh well Shirl, it will probably clean up just fine."

"I sure hope so. The darn coat cost me a couple hundred bucks which is more than I can really afford."

"Oh heck, Shirley, what is money? It is just lying around in stacks over at the bank."

"Yes I saw. Can you fix me up with a stack or two?"

"Well, Shirley, my dear, I could but I don't relish the thought of spending the rest of my life in jail."

"Let's have another manhattan, order a porterhouse steak and make believe we are rich," said Shirley.

"I don't know, Shirl, these are very good manhattans but another one might be more than I can handle. What the heck, let's do it! We only live once. We have not had a chance for a lot of girl talk for quite a while."

"Geez, Betty, wouldn't it be great if we were rich. We could have an apartment in New York, a villa on the Riviera, limos, servants and you name it."

"Dream on gal. I'm afraid it will never happen."

They started on the third manhattan and were getting a little tipsy.

"Betty, I have a little secret I will share if you promise not to tell a soul."

"Of course I won't tell. You know me. We have had secrets before. Don't tell me you are pregnant."

"No nothing like that. I was down in the sub-basement the other day and discovered there is a secret tunnel to the bank building. A big steam pipe runs through it. The tunnel is just big enough to let me skinny through. It goes to the bank building basement and then there is a stairway leading to a closet right off the lobby not far from where you work. I took the tunnel over today and that is how I got my coat dirty. It rubbed against the steam pipe."

"No kidding! Wow, you mean if someone robbed the bank they could escape through the tunnel and out through the Soo Line building?"

"Yup, what do you think of them bananas, Betty?"

"Very interesting indeed. Perhaps we could figure out a way to get rich at that."

"Betty, what are you thinking?"

"Just pipe dreaming, Shirl. Let's have a grasshopper and head for home."

Edwards' Family Problems

Chicago, IL
Dear Johnny,

Thank you for the money you sent. I know you work hard and save so we do appreciate everything you do. Times are very difficult here since we moved. The company cut back and your Dad is working only three days a week now. We have had some expense with the house and problems with the car. Your grandfather has been helping too and we do appreciate that. Your Dad has been looking for a better job but at his age, good jobs are hard to find. I wish we were back in New Brighton so we could be near you. You are a good son.

Love Always,
Mom

Johnny was very depressed by the letter from his mother. He wondered what he could do to help. He wondered if he should quit school and find a full time job. He pondered the possibility of getting away with robbing the bank. His mind went in circles as he tried to come up with a plan.

The following days found Johnny spending as much time as he could in the cavern under the bank vault. He worked diligently at cutting a hole through the ceiling of the cavern under the vault. He would no doubt have to do some blasting to get through it.

⇥ Sarah Called Bob ⇤

"HI, BOB. THIS IS Sarah from Hinkley. How are you?"

"Just fine Sarah. What's up?"

"Are you alone, Bob? I need to talk to you confidentially."

"Yes. What's on your mind?"

"We have had a private investigator here and he was checking on all the robberies at the Oasis stations. He took me aside and asked a lot of questions about the holdup here. The police had gathered some information right after the robbery and turned it over to him. He suspects that whoever did it might come back to the store and I should keep an eye out for anyone who I think resembles the robber. He said they found footprints from size ten shoes having bearclaw tread with particles of sandstone from them. I had told the police I thought the robber had two different colored eyes so that too was part of the record."

"Oh, so they are still working on that case?"

"Yes, Bob, and of course they have had a couple similar robberies and they think it might be the same person. They are offering a big reward and trying hard to catch the guy."

"How can I help, Sarah?"

"Bob, I have been thinking a lot about this and you will recall we noted that your friend Johnny had two different eye colors. He was in the area hunting with your party at the time of the holdup. He seemed like such a nice guy, I hate to think he could have been involved. But I'm telling you this secretly so perhaps you can give it some thought and come up with a reason to eliminate him from my mind. I don't want it to be him but I keep seeing his eyes."

"Well, Sarah, I don't know what to say. Johnny would never do something like that. He's been my friend for a long time. He's an honorable guy and he was out in the woods hunting with us at the time of the holdup."

"Okay, Bob thanks a lot. I like him, too. It's just been gnawing at me. I will try to stop thinking of him."

⚔ Johnny's Missing ⚔

BOB DECIDED TO GIVE Johnny a call and get together for lunch the next day. Johnny did not answer the phone so Bob left a message suggesting lunch at the Nankin at noon.

Johnny did not return the call, so Bob called again the following day. There was still no response from Johnny. Thinking this was quite strange, Bob went to Johnny's apartment. He arrived to find lights on in the apartment. He rang the doorbell repeatedly. There was no response. There were newspapers at the door and mail in the mailbox.

It appeared the door was locked with a simple skeleton key. Bob had a key so went inside calling for Johnny. Bob checked the entire apartment. Johnny was not there. Although old, the apartment was neat and clean. A desk calendar on the desk indicated it had not been turned to the correct date for a couple of days. Bob had a strange feeling about it but decided Johnny must have gone somewhere for a few days. Bob put the papers and the mail on the desk and left.

He phoned Shirley and Betty and found they had not heard from Johnny either. He discovered Johnny's class schedule and determined that Johnny had not attended classes for several days. Seeing Johnny's address book, Bob phoned Johnny's parents and grandfather. No one was aware of Johnny's whereabouts. Bob went down to the police station and filed a missing person's report.

Bob was very concerned about Johnny's absence. He returned to the apartment again the following day to search for clues. In the top drawer of the desk, he found a spiral notebook containing sketches and numbered markings. As he studied the drawings he noted precise figures for distances, angles and elevations that didn't seem to make sense. Then, on another page, he found references to a storm sewer and caverns. Bob knew that Johnny was very interested in the caves under the city but he had not been mentioning anything about them lately. After scrutinizing the sketches, he began to realize the storm sewer referred to the big one a short ways from Johnny's apartment.

It suddenly dawned on him that something could have happened to Johnny underground. Bob contacted the city engineering department and obtained the assistance of an engineer who was familiar with the system of storm sewers. With the sketch book in hand, they entered the storm sewer and followed it to a point marked in Johnny's book as an opening. The engineer noted the hole in the brick wall was newly made and should not have been there. They peered into the hole and saw a cavern extending away from the wall. Shining a floodlight into the cavern they noted a pile of rock which had apparently fallen from the roof of the cavern.

Bob peered in, shined his floodlight on the pile of rock and felt faint.

"Oh my God, I see a shoe."

The engineer looked carefully and he saw it, too. They called the fire department special services group. The rock was moved aside and the body was removed from the cavern.

It was evident a large chunk of rock had fallen from the ceiling crushing Johnny's chest. Bob could detect the faint odor of explosive, but said nothing. He noticed that Johnny's shoes had the bearclaw tread that the Hinkley police were looking for. That was another observation he would keep to himself.

The lead fireman called the police and an officer soon arrived to investigate the situation. They all questioned what Johnny could be doing in the cave. Bob explained that he and Johnny had an interest in the caves and tunnels under the city and no doubt Johnny was simply doing a little more exploring. Bob told them about some of the caves they had explored and about a few other individuals who had also done similar exploring.

The investigating officer seemed to accept the explanation. Combining the notes in the spiral notebook and the faint smell of explosive, Bob had thoughts of another reason for Johnny being in the cave but he decided keep these thoughts to himself. He destroyed the spiral notebook. He decided there were some secrets that would die with his friend Johnny.

Bob instructed that the body be taken to the morgue until he could notify Johnny's parents. Distraught and barely able to talk he called the Edwards.

"Mr. Edwards, this is Bob Nason, a friend of Johnny's. I am sorry to tell you I have some very bad news. I am sure you are aware that Johnny had a great interest in the caves under the city. Well, there has been an accidental cave-in and Johnny was crushed under a large rock. We have recovered the body and it is being held at the city morgue awaiting your advice. I am so sorry sir. Johnny was my best friend. It is a terrible loss."

"Oh my God, how in the world did that happen?"

"We aren't sure sir. It appears Johnny was simply at the wrong place at the wrong time. For some reason this large chunk of rock came loose from the ceiling of the cavern and fell directly on him."

"Well, Mrs. Edwards and I will get a flight from O'Hare as soon as we can." Bob heard the anguish in Mr. Edwards's voice.

"If you let me know what flight you will be on, I will be happy to meet you at the airport and then take you around as necessary for you to make the arrangements."

"Thank you, Bob. We will certainly appreciate that."

Bob met the Edwards when they arrived at the airport that evening and took them to his parents' home to spend the night. The next day he took them to the morgue and then helped them make arrangements for cremation. They arranged for services and burial at St. John the Baptist Catholic Church in New Brighton.

Betty knew Johnny had a safe deposit box at the First National Bank. She suggested that Mr. Edwards remove the contents. To the surprise of everyone, it contained a life insurance policy Johnny had bought some time ago naming his parents as beneficiaries. The policy would pay a benefit of one hundred thousand dollars. In addition, there was a handwritten will bequeathing all of his personal belongings to his parents. An unexplained curiosity in the box was the steel head of a nine pound maul. That would forever remain a mystery.

The church was filled for Johnny's funeral. It was a painful day for the Edwards, but they were comforted to be surrounded by many of their old friends from the neighborhood.

That evening they made a decision that would change their lives forever. After a lengthy discussion with Grandpa Ed and Mable, they decided to move back to the area and occasionally help in the operation of the farm.

⚛ After the Funeral ⚛

BOB, BETTY AND SHIRLEY got together for dinner a few days after Johnny's funeral. They were all feeling low after losing their long-time friend.

Shirley was almost in tears and said, "I miss him so much. We didn't get together all that much lately, but we were close. He wanted us to take a long trip together as soon as he saved up enough money. He said he had a plan that could make us very rich. He never did explain the plan to me but he seemed very serious about it."

Bob said, "I wish we had a plan to make us rich. It is tough just trying to keep up with the bills these days."

Betty remarked, "Well I see plenty of it every day in the vault but unfortunately none of it is mine."

Bob asked, "Well theoretically, just how hard would it be to get some of that money?"

Betty responded, "Getting it would be easy enough but getting away with it would be the problem."

Shirley asked, "Wouldn't it be wonderful to take off on a trip around the world? We could go together and see Rome, Paris the Orient and even Australia. Johnny and I talked about it. Too bad his plan didn't work out."

Bob said, "My God, what are we talking about, robbing the bank? Nobody gets away with that."

They laughed and agreed that they'd better come up with a better idea to get rich. Taking a trip together however would be a wonderful idea. They toasted to doing that together ---- someday.

Bob continued his studies at the university. Shirley continued working at the Soo Line and Betty stayed at the bank part-time. Shirley and Betty got together for dinner after work frequently. Dinner usually included a few drinks.

"You know Betty, I can't stop dreaming about all that money in the vault over at your bank and the wonderful time we could have with it. My pipe dreams have been fantastic."

"I can understand that, my friend, but does your dream include a lifetime in prison?"

"Yes, I know Betty, but let me dream a little."

"Okay Shirley, let's have another drink and you tell me all about your dream."

"Okay, it goes like this. You told me you know the workings of the locks on the vault doors, right? So, I could come over just before you went off duty and I would bring a large brief case. You could show me how to operate the door locks from the inside, lock me in the vault and leave for the day as usual. I would fill my briefcase with greenbacks, wait about an hour to be sure everyone had left the bank and then slip out of the vault and into the tunnel to the Soo Line sub basement. From there it would be a breeze to go up the stairs to the lobby level and outside. I know the watchman in the lobby. He makes rounds to check doors on a couple of floors and is gone for at least a half hour. The guards change shifts on a regular schedule and while they are busy, I could stroll out to Marquette Avenue and we are away free."

"Oh my God! You're serious, aren't you!"

"Think about it. We could arrange to have Bob pick us up and maybe go to his cabin until things cool off and make plans from there. This would work really well over a long holiday weekend. We could be out of the country before the bank figured out the money was missing."

"Wow, Shirley, it sounds like you have been dreaming the same dream for some time."

"Well, what do you think? Does that sound like it could work?"

"Shirley, I really get scared just thinking about it. Yes, it might be workable, but your dream doesn't include what happens if we get caught!"

"Well, just think about it, Betty. I know things could go wrong but if it worked out, we would be done working for the rest of our lives."

"I don't think Bob would go along with something like that Shirl."

"Well, he really would not have to know about it until it was all over. We could just tell him to pick us up and take us to his cabin for an outing. You could arrange that with him couldn't you?"

"Oh, I guess so."

"Okay, Betty, think it over. Time to go home. Why don't you sleep on it?"

The girls met frequently and each time discussed the plan. Shirley was quite serious about it. Betty had serious reservations. At a later dinner meeting, Shirley really pressed Betty.

"Did you see that Christmas falls on a Friday this year?"

"Yes, I know, Shirl."

"Well, the bank will probably close early on Christmas Eve, be closed on Friday, Saturday and Sunday. If we would do our thing on the 24th, the bank wouldn't be aware of it until some time on Monday the 28th. We would have more than three days to make our get-away."

⇥ The Act ⇤

FINALLY CONVINCED, BETTY TAUGHT Shirley how to manipulate the vault locks. This took several visits as Shirley could not spend much time at the vault on each visit without causing suspicion. She had to make it appear she was just stopping in to greet Betty.

They made plans for Bob to pick them up at the parking lot near the old Milwaukee Road Depot on the evening of December 24th. He would park there for free and it was near a convenient bus stop. Shirley had worked out all the remaining details and the plan.

December 24th arrived. Betty had prepared to go off duty. Shirley arrived and slipped quietly into the vault. Betty closed the vault and left. She walked out and up to the corner at Marquette Street.

Shirley waited inside the vault with her large brief case and listened. She heard the air conditioning fan shut down. She could feel there was no more fresh air being pumped into the vault and the lights dimmed. She knew then that the guard had left the lobby and went to check other floors.

Shirley let herself out of the vault carefully, quickly looked around the lobby and hurried to the closet and down the stairway to the tunnel. She crossed to the Soo Line Building sub-basement and started up the stairs to the basement. Just then, she noticed the elevator had stopped at the sub-basement level.

A janitor emerged. Shirley dashed up the stairs to the basement level and ran up the next stair to the lobby. She peeked out the stairway door and saw the evening lobby guard already seated at his desk. Her timing was off. She checked her watch. He could not have patrolled the upper floor yet. She waited, breathing heavily as she peered through the tiny crack of the slightly opened door. She couldn't take a chance on leaving and having the guard see her. Betty would be waiting for her outside and Bob would be waiting at the parking lot. She was nervous and perspiring now.

Suddenly there was a change! A data processing clerk arrived, apparently late for work. The guard had him sign in and then accompanied him up the elevator to the computer room. Shirley made a dash for it and ran out the doors to Marquette Street.

Betty was waiting at the bus stop but the bus was not there. They both hurried north on Marquette to the next bus stop. They waited anxiously. When it arrived, they hopped on and rode to the parking lot where Bob was waiting in his car. They tossed their bags into the trunk and were on their way. Bob was unaware that he was an accomplice to a robbery. He headed for the family cabin expecting a weekend of fun with the girls.

Disaster

WHEN THEY ARRIVED, BOB parked the car behind a grove of trees a short way from the cabin and told the girls to go in. He said he would get the luggage after opening up the cabin.

As soon as he entered the building, Bob could smell fuel oil. He went over to the closet near the fireplace, opened the door and noticed that a five-gallon can of fuel oil had been leaking from one of the shelves. The can was on a shelf a few feet above the floor. The fuel oil had run along the shelf and dripped down onto a bag of fertilizer and then run out onto the floor toward the fireplace. The bag appeared saturated with fuel oil. Bob sensed the danger immediately. He ran out the side door intending to get a scoop shovel and pail with which to haul the wet explosive mess outside.

Shirley fumbled in the dim light until she found a kerosene lamp and matches on the fireplace mantel. Unaware of anything unusual, she lit the lamp and threw the matchstick toward the fireplace. The oil on the floor immediately ignited and the flame raced to the oil-soaked fertilizer.

WHAMMO!!! The bag exploded with the force of an enormous bomb. The girls were both killed instantly as the blast blew the building apart. In seconds the scene became a burning inferno. Bob had been running back to the cabin from the tool shed. The force of the explosion blew him off the ground and into a pile of brush.

A neighbor heard the blast and called the fire department. Several units arrived and fought the blaze, but it was too late to save anything. Later that night, when the fire had been extinguished, the coroner removed the charred remains of the two girls.

Bob miraculously survived with only contusions, cuts, scratches and a terrific headache. The local fire department notified the county sheriff who arranged for the remains to be taken to the Pine County Morgue.

After paramedics treated Bob's head, he provided as much information as he could to the sheriff. Bob then went to a motel in Hinkley. He called his parents to tell them of the tragedy. He was grateful that the local authorities would be notifying the girls' parents. He would speak with them later, but then, completely exhausted, he went to bed.

⤳ Surprise ⤶

I T WAS AFTER NOON on Christmas Day before Bob awoke. His head was pounding as he drove back home to New Brighton. While removing his suitcase from the trunk of his car he noticed Shirley's bulging briefcase. He opened it and almost fainted. It was packed full of large denomination bills. He immediately sensed that something was terribly wrong.

Where had this money come from? Who did it belong to? Shirley's initials were on the briefcase and there were papers inside which identified it as hers. Questions raced through his mind. Was it real money? Where did Shirley get it? Who else knew about it? What should he do with it? Even in his current state of pain and fatigue, he realized things would only get worse unless he turned this in to the authorities. After a great deal of difficulty he was able to reach the sheriff personally.

"Hello, Sheriff, I'm sorry to be interrupting your Christmas Day, but I have a situation which I believe deserves your personal attention. It's pretty important. Can we meet this afternoon?"

"What's so important that one of my deputies can't help you out?"

"Sheriff, it involves a great amount of money and I think it would be to your advantage to deal with it now. I am sure you and your department will certainly become involved on Monday morning. Discussing this with you personally today would no doubt be to your advantage."

"Alright. You better be right about this. Meet me at headquarters in my office on South Third Street in forty- five minutes. And don't be late."

"You won't regret this. I will be there. Thank you very much."

When Bob opened the briefcase on the Sheriff's desk, the Sheriff let out a low whistle.

"There must be a couple hundred thousand here. OK, where'd you get it?"

Bob explained the events of the previous day and how the friends had once joked about robbing a bank.

"Sheriff, I found this briefcase in the trunk of my car this morning after returning from a horrible experience up at Hinkley where my parent's cabin exploded and killed two girls. They had arranged for me to take them to the cabin and we were to spend the weekend there. This bag obviously belonged to Shirley Nolan who worked at the Soo Line. The other girl was Betty Hanson who worked part-time at the First National Bank, primarily in the area near the vault. I do not know where they got the money but I am certainly suspicious it could be from First National. They were both friends of mine. We all lived in New Brighton and went to

Highview High together. Sheriff, I would like to turn this money over to you and suggest that you make a discreet inquiry with First National as soon as possible and keep the matter as quiet as possible for the sake of the parents and for the reputations of the girls."

"I'm not sure I can offer them any protection. If they did rob the bank, it's out of my control."

Bob raised an eyebrow and stared into the sheriff's eyes.

"This happened under your watch, Sheriff. If I were the president of a bank that got robbed by two young girls, I might not think that law enforcement was doing such a good job."

"Well Bob, I am happy you brought this to my personal attention. This department has a vested interest in the protection and safety of all of our banks. I will contact the President of First National immediately. I'm sure the vault is locked but perhaps he has a way of entry and the ability to make an accounting even today or tomorrow. And, from a safety perspective, I can see that we must all keep this very confidential as you suggest. Thank you very much Bob. I will keep in touch."

"And thank you for coming out today sir. I hope I didn't make you late for Christmas dinner."

The sheriff called Bob early Monday morning asking him to return to Headquarters. Bob was a bit uncertain about the sheriff's motives, but needed to follow through on behalf of his friends.

When he arrived, both the bank president and the sheriff greeted him with handshakes and smiles. They had determined how the money had been obtained and had confirmed that it had all been returned. The case was solved. The sheriff presented Bob with an award for meritorious service and the bank president offered him a certified check in the amount of five thousand dollars as a reward. They agreed that, under the circumstances, this case would be considered closed and no word of it would be given to the media. Bob was astounded.

"Gentlemen, I thank you both very much. It is sad indeed that my friends were responsible and that they came to such a tragic end. I must say I go with a very heavy heart."

The Sheriff said, "Bob, we understand."

Bob returned home satisfied he had done the right thing with the money but filled with sadness at the loss of two more very dear friends.

The remains of the two girls were cremated and there was a joint funeral for them at St. John the Baptist Church. The large church was filled to capacity with mourners paying their respects for these two young people.

⚞ Vision at Cemetery ⚟

MONTHS LATER, BOB SAT on a bench in the cemetery. It was summer now. The tragedies of the past year were behind him. An occasional zephyr passing through among the plantings and markers was the only sound except for the rumble of the highway off in the distance.

His friends were buried here. There was so much to remember. There was no further investigation of the tunnel where Johnny had died and no more station robberies. There was so much he must try to forget. There were secrets he must never divulge. He would visit here often.

Bob sat silently for a long time viewing, from a distance, the graves of his friends. After a while, he found himself concentrating on Betty Hanson's gravestone. It was white marble, about three feet tall and slightly shaded from the afternoon sun by a nearby maple tree. He rested against the back of the bench, his eyes partially closed and his mind deeply in thought of times past when all at once he was startled to see Betty take form, resting on her stone. She was dressed in a long white gown, her blond tresses adorning her face and she seemed to be smiling directly at him.

Bob was frightened and alarmed. He couldn't believe what he was seeing. He opened his eyes and jumped to his feet just as she disappeared into thin air. Trembling, he walked over to the stone and rubbed his eyes to be sure he was wide awake. He looked around to see if there was anyone else in the cemetery. Bewildered, he wondered if he was losing his mind. The vision was too real to be disregarded.

He went back to the bench, waited and watched to see if the vision would reappear. Bob really loved Betty. They had had so many good times together. He recalled the senior prom and the first time they kissed. He recalled the auto accident following the prom, the many wonderful days on the river. He knew had she lived, they would most certainly have become married. She was on his mind almost every minute of every day.

One thing he could not understand was how she could have become involved in the bank robbery. It just wasn't like her. There was no need for her to be a party to that terrible deed as far as he could determine. It must have been Shirley's idea. It seemed completely out of character for either of those girls. Could it have been just a lark, a dare or was there some deep unknown reason for them to want that amount of money.

He waited for an hour or more, but the vision did not reappear. He wondered what had happened here. This was completely beyond his comprehension. He left the cemetery and went home very confused. He knew he could not discuss this with anyone or they would certainly question his sanity. As a matter of fact, he wasn't sure himself.

After supper he went for a long walk around the lake reviewing the events of the day. He could not come up with any logical explanation for what he had seen. He said to himself, "*Oh God, if I could only hold her in my arms again.*"

Bob stayed up late reading. He was not tired but finally went to bed. Unable to sleep he arose about one o'clock. He dressed, slipped out of the house and drove back to the cemetery. It was a clear, warm starlit night. He felt strangely comfortable sitting there on the bench looking at that marble headstone. He told himself he must certainly be losing his mind to be doing what he was doing. To sit in a dark cemetery in the middle of the night was certainly insanity. He sat there for about an hour and returned home. His head was aching and bursting with thoughts of Betty.

Arising the next morning after a fitful sleepless night, Bob remembered he wanted to go downtown and shop for a few items. He dressed, had a light breakfast and drove downtown. He parked in a ramp and started walking toward the mall. A bus came along going the same direction he was walking. He watched as the bus was passing him and to his complete amazement, there in a window looking directly at him and smiling a big broad smile, was Betty.

He ran, following the bus hoping he could board at the next stop. The bus reached the next stop before he could catch it. Running as fast as he could, he watched as Betty stepped off the bus, looked in his direction and slipped around the corner and out of sight.

He ran to the corner, nearly out of breath, looked down the street but she was nowhere to be seen. Completely dismayed, he walked over to the Mall, sat on a bench and tried to catch his breath and understand what was happening.

He wondered if he was seeing ghosts, having hallucinations or losing his mind. All at once, he felt a slight breeze that passed momentarily. It was as if he were being given a message. He felt a strange momentary shiver throughout his body and then depression.

He was becoming emotionally unstable and started crying quietly to himself. He decided to forget the shopping. He walked back to the ramp and drove toward home. He drove up Silver Lake Road, turned off and headed for the cemetery. He parked and walked in to Betty's gravestone.

"What are you doing to me?" he yelled. "I love you but you have to leave me alone now."

He returned to his car and sat there sobbing. After regaining his composure he decided he needed to be alone and go for a long walk.

He returned home and told his parents he was going up north. Bob headed toward Hinkley, his mind fully engrossed with thoughts of Betty, the recent events and his state of mind.

He stopped at the Oasis and had a cup of coffee. The store was not busy so he and Sarah took the opportunity to talk. Bob told her he was going up to the burned-out cabin and then take a long walk in the woods.

Sarah had known Bob for a long time and could see he was not himself.

She said, "Bob, you will be walking right past here on your way down. Stop in and I will buy you a sandwich and coffee."

"Thanks Sarah, I might just do that. Thanks."

Bob left and drove up to the burned out cottage. All that remained was a charred mess of rubble and boards leaning up against the blackened stone fireplace chimney. He walked around to the backside and sat on an old metal lawn chair that had escaped the destruction. Resting there he tried to identify some of the burned objects. He could see remnants of a couple guns, some cooking utensils, a water pail and a few other similar items.

Then, his body shivered, she appeared! She stood, standing ghostlike in front of the fireplace, intermingled with the charred boards and debris but aglow as the sunlight beamed upon her in a shaft of light passing between the branches of a huge tree. Bob was stunned.

He yelled out, "I didn't mean to kill you. It was an accident."

He covered his eyes with his hands, lowered his head and started sobbing. "I'm so sorry. I loved you so much!" He raised his head and opened his eyes. She was gone.

He sat there crying and talking to himself. *"If I had only told the girls to run out of the cabin while I was after the shovel, they might have escaped. If I had not kept the fertilizer and fuel oil in the same location it wouldn't have happened. It was stupid to have both stored in that closet. God, I know it was my fault but I didn't want it to happen. It was an accident."* He rambled on in his grief, feeling sorry for the girls and himself.

Distraught, he got up, walked to the trail and started walking south along the edge of the woods. He knew he had to pull himself together. He knew his current condition of grief, guilt and hallucinations could end up in his suicide. He walked and ran sometimes yelling to himself as he proceeded along the trail.

The coolness of the shaded woods had a somewhat soothing effect on him and he became more rational as he continued on his way. Squirrels watched from the treetops and he noted a couple of deer behind a patch of blackberry brush as he passed by. The quiet of the forest was broken occasionally by the raucous caw of a crow as it flew overhead alerting the forest animals of Bob's presence.

Bob knew the woods well having spent many pleasurable days here over the years. He was now hoping its calm and serenity would help him through this terrible emotional upheaval in his life.

Bob followed the path along the east edge of the forest until he reached the station. He had settled down quite well by this time, so he decided to take Sarah up on her offer of a sandwich and coffee.

Sarah had been expecting him. She ushered him to a table in the rear of the store and brought a couple cups of coffee and some sandwiches and offered him a choice. He selected one and they proceeded with their lunch and conversation.

"I'm glad you came back. You seem a little down. Talk to me."

"Well Sarah, I've had better times. Losing my friends and the cabin has all been a bitter blow."

"You've gone through a lot, Bob. Give yourself some time to recover."

"But Sarah, I'm the one to blame for the explosion. That oil and fertilizer should never have been in that closet. We kept it there for years but that was a mistake. It was a horrible mistake and I should have known better. Dad should have known better too. But the damage is done. There's no going back."

"Don't blame yourself Bob. Bad things happen to good people, too. No matter how hard we try to do everything right. We all know it was not intentional."

"You're very kind Sarah, but this is something I could have prevented. It's a sin of omission. I could have stored the fuel oil outside away from the fertilizer. Also I could have told the girls to get out of the cabin as soon as I smelled the fuel oil, and saw the damp bag. I didn't recognize the danger as being that imminent. These are things I am going to have to live with for the rest of my life."

"I understand what you are saying Bob but you cannot carry a load of guilt like that around for the rest of your life. What has happened, happened. Call it God's will or fate or whatever but you know it was not something you intended to happen."

"Sarah, thank you for trying to help. You are a good friend."

"Yes, we have been friends for a long time and I have a question I would like to ask you. Maybe it's not the right time."

"No, please. What is it??"

"It's about Johnny. I know he was a friend of yours and he seemed like a wonderful guy. I know he's gone and maybe it shouldn't matter, but was he the guy that held me up and robbed the store?"

"Sarah, I loved Johnny like a brother and it pains me that he is gone. Honestly, what difference does it make now?"

"I know this is a really bad time to put any more on your shoulders, but I have to ask. I slept with Johnny and now I have missed a couple of periods! I may be carrying his baby. I need to know."

"Oh my God! I don't know what to think or say."

"Be a friend and just tell me what you know. I hope you can see why it is important to me."

"Of course, Sarah. I understand but I do not have a positive answer. All I can do is tell you what I know and sincerely hope you will keep it a secret."

"Bob, you know I can keep a secret."

"Well, here goes. Johnny was hunting with us the day you were robbed. I gave him the four-wheeler and asked him to come down the trail along the east side of the woods and then come back north and try to drive any deer north to us as we stood at the north end waiting for the deer to come through. I have thought about this quite a bit and I figure Johnny should have arrived here at about the time you were held up. He came through on the drive and he did seem quite nervous however nothing was said. I found out later he was in need of money. When we found Johnny in the cave where he died, he was wearing shoes of the size and tread type that made marks on the floor here and they had the same type of sand granules that were found on the floor here too. The sand granules were the type found in the cave. Johnny's eyes were, in fact, each a different color as you girls noted when you were at the cabin. As far as I am concerned it all adds up, however it is all circumstantial. This was all my secret and now you, alone, share it."

"Wow, what a story. Thank you for telling me. I am going to the doctor tomorrow for a pregnancy test. If it comes up positive, I don't know what I will do. I haven't figured out my options if I am pregnant by a dead man --- that will be something."

"Let's hope that is not the case. Call me tomorrow night to let me know what you find out."

"Thanks, Bob. Wish me luck!"

"I will, Sarah. Now I guess I had better get hiking or I won't make it back to my car before dark. Thank you for the lunch."

"Okay, Bob, and I wish you luck, too."

Bob left and continued his trek through the woods. It was late afternoon by the time he reached the cabin and his car. He sat in the lawn chair to rest a bit. As the sun set the forest darkened. Bob was overtaken by an eerie feeling as he viewed the burned out structure. He wondered if he would again see the image of Betty appear. He had strange mixed feelings of fear and yet comfort at the thought of seeing her. He was afraid of how he was being affected by these sightings and yet felt a sort of comfort and longing. They were feelings he had never had before and could not explain.

As he sat there he wished she would appear again. The forest became dark and the blackened burned out building blended in with the nightfall until only darkness was visible. A slight breeze picked up and dampness settled in. It was time to leave.

Bob arose and started walking back to his car. When he walked past the structure he thought he saw a flash of a bluish white light near the fireplace. He stopped, looked back and saw nothing. He felt very alone and somewhat frightened as he proceeded to his car and left.

Alone on the road, Bob headed for home, stopped at "Toby's" for supper, and then continued on. As he drove, he wondered about his future. He wondered if the visions would continue forever. He wondered what he could do about it. He also wondered about Sarah. What if she were pregnant? If so, was it his fault for having her stay over that night and approved of her sleeping with Johnny? Could he be blamed for them having sex at his cabin? The problems mounted in his mind.

It was late when he arrived home but he decided he must have a talk with his parents. The three of them gathered in the living room and Bob explained his visions of Betty and how it was affecting him. They were understanding and sympathetic. They all agreed it might be good for Bob to leave the area for a while. Perhaps if he were away from these surroundings, so familiar to both he and Betty the visions might stop. If he would become involved with other things and other people his mind might be distracted from thoughts of her.

Bob decided he would take leave from his job, take a break from school and go on an extended vacation. The following day he packed up his clothes and bid farewell to his saddened parents not knowing where he was going or when he might return.

⚞ Heading North ⚟

BOB HEADED NORTH FROM the Twin Cities. He had no destination in mind. He just wanted to leave. He wanted to find peace and quiet. He wanted to escape all the sorrowful reminders that surrounded him there and perhaps start a new life. He wanted to clear his cluttered mind of the bombardment of unhappy thoughts so pervasive in his existence during these recent months.

Driving through the countryside brought out some mental relief. There was an inner feeling of freedom difficult for him to understand. After an hour or so he stopped at a small country restaurant for coffee and a donut. The diner had only three small tables and a short counter. He sat at the counter. The only other occupant was the young waitress who was tending the place.

She was young, pretty and friendly so they struck up conversation immediately. Their lighthearted conversation soon led to jokes and laughter. He thought, *God it feels good to laugh.*

He couldn't remember when he had last laughed really hard. He touched his face with his hand because it somehow seemed different on the outside. He felt tears of laughter. It felt good. He lingered over his coffee, relishing the change. "Goodbye, handsome. Y'all come back soon."

Back on the road, he felt refreshed and eager to be on with the new change in his life. He continued northward taking secondary roads, enjoying the scenery. He got lost on dead ends a couple of times but it didn't matter. He finally he ended up in Duluth, Minnesota.

He found a restaurant and a motel and settled in for the night. It had been a day of many mixed feelings. There had been sadness in leaving his home and parents, the feeling of escape, freedom and the open road, laughter and the strangeness of being in a new city. Then he remembered he had promised to call Sarah.

⚛ Sarah Visits Doctor ⚛

Sarah took the forenoon off and drove to the Pine City Clinic. She was able to get right in to see Dr. Brown. It was quite embarrassing, but she knew she had to find out if she was pregnant or not.

It didn't take long before she was called into the smiling doctor's office. He was not aware that she was unmarried when he came out and announced, "Congratulations, you are going to become a mother."

Sarah bowed her head and sighed.

"Can you tell how far along I am doctor?"

The doctor looked at her chart. He asked a lot of embarrassing questions about her menstrual cycle and sexual intercourse. She finally told him that she was not married and this was the result having had sex only the one time. He was very understanding and explained that these things happen all the time. He finally told her it appeared she was about two months along.

"Well, Doctor, is there still time to get an abortion?"

"Sarah, I do not perform abortions, nor do I recommend them, but to answer your question, yes it is still possible from a time standpoint."

"Thank you, Doctor, I'm afraid I am in quite a bind."

"Sorry, Sarah, I wish you the best. If I can be of further help let me know."

Sarah returned to the store and finished her day at work. It was a difficult day. Her mind was not on her work. She struggled to think what her options might be. She knew there were abortion clinics in the city but was reluctant to take that way out.

Bob had said he would call her that evening. She decided she would discuss it with Bob when he called. Maybe he would have other thoughts. Oh God, what if he offered to marry her? Fat chance, she thought to herself.

It was almost nine o'clock when Bob finally reached Sarah. He described his trip, explained he had driven up to Duluth and told her briefly that he was taking a little vacation to try and clear the cobwebs from his mind. She didn't fully understand but related to him the events of her day.

"Bob, I went to the doctor today and found out I am pregnant. I just can't believe I could be pregnant from having sex just once with Johnny. But he said I am about two months along. I have not had relations with anyone except Johnny that night at your cabin. I am now in a real pickle. I don't like any of the options I can think of. I suppose I could take care of it quickly with an abortion, but I am not much in favor of that. I don't think I want to raise a kid conceived in a one night stand. Do you have any bright ideas?"

"Geez, Sarah, I'm sorry you're going through this. You know I thought about this on my drive today and I do have a suggestion."

Sarah brightened, "You do?"

"It is so sad that Johnny is gone but it is just possible his parents, who are the grandparents of the child, might just have an interest. I know them. They are fine people. As strange as this might seem to you, I recommend that you visit them, explain the situation and solicit their recommendations."

"You want me to go and tell them I had a one-night stand with their dead son?"

"Yes, Sarah, I think they are probably very understanding and compassionate people. Regardless of your decision, it would be good to have them share in it."

"Boy, I don't know. That would be difficult for me to do. I appreciate your trying to help, but don't you think they would be upset, or look down on me or think I was after them for something?

"No, they are good people. I am sure you would not regret it."

"Who are his parents and where do they live?"

"They are Fred and Emily Edwards and they live at 1917 Highview Drive, New Brighton.

Sarah felt doubtful. "I don't know, Bob. Don't I come off as the bad girl?"

"The Edwards just moved back from Chicago to their old neighborhood. It is a little complicated, but I think they are settled in by now. If you like I can call them and tell them that you are a friend of Johnny's and you'd like to see them."

"Well, okay, but don't tell them why I am coming. Let me break it to them gently."

"When can you be there?"

"I will lay off work and plan to be there about one o'clock tomorrow if that is okay with them."

"I will call them and call you right back."

Bob called her back in a few minutes.

"Okay, it is all set. I told them you were a friend of mine and had met Johnny up at the cabin. You are going to be in the cities and would like to meet Johnny's parents.

They will be happy to see you. I will call you tomorrow night to see how it works out."

"Thanks much, Bob, I appreciate your help."

"Good night, Sarah. I will talk to you tomorrow night."

❦ Sarah Visits the Edwards ❧

SARAH HESITATED BEFORE RINGING the doorbell. It was opened by a small woman with a ready smile.

"Good afternoon, Mrs. Edwards? My name is Sarah Williams. I am a friend of Bob Nason."

"Good afternoon, Sarah. Bob told us to expect you. Please come in and meet Mr. Edwards, and please call us Emily and Fred."

Sarah was escorted to the living room and met Fred. Both Emily and Fred appeared to be in their late 40's or early 50's. Their home appeared to be quite comfortable and was a nicely furnished middle class home. Emily apologized that they were not fully settled since their recent return, but they were happy to be back with old friends after the loss of their son.

"Yes, I can well imagine how difficult it must be for you. I, too, am very sorry he is gone. That's why I came to see you. I am not sure how to begin telling you the reason for my visit. This is all so very embarrassing. I guess I should start from the beginning."

"Yes, please do, dear," Emily replied.

Sarah nervously relayed how she works at the Oasis, met Johnny at Bob's party at the cabin, and had a wonderful time eating and drinking and dancing.

"I have known the Nasons for several years. They stop at the station for supplies while spending time at the cabin. Well, on this particular weekend Bob and Johnny were at the cabin. Bob called the store and asked me to come up after work and bring some pizzas and drinks. I took my friend Mary along. We all got acquainted, had pizza and drinks and then Bob brought out a tape player so we danced and had a really good time. Johnny and I became real friendly and--- I am sorry to admit, we slept together."

Fred asked, "Are you saying this was the first time you ever met Johnny and yet you slept with him?"

Sarah stammered, "Yes, Yes. I am ashamed to admit it, but it's true. I assure you sir, I do not go around having sex with men. Johnny just seemed so special. We were having such a good time and we had been drinking quite a bit. It just happened. And now I find I am pregnant."

"What?" --- Fred rose in dismay.

"Please believe me! It was the very first time I ever had sex and I still don't understand how I let my guard down, even with Johnny. He was so loving and gentle. I just cuddled up to him and it just happened and now he is gone." Sarah cried openly.

Emily handed her some tissues.

Fred said gruffly, "Hmph. A likely story. So what has this got to do with us?"

Sarah buried her face in her hands bowed her head and covered her eyes with a handkerchief as she cried softly. She hesitated a few moments before being able to speak again.

"I understand you are upset but even though I knew Johnny for only the one night, I wanted to meet you. I felt it would be helpful in deciding what to do about the pregnancy. I wanted to know what Johnny's family was like. Bob and I have been friends a long time and he thinks the world of you. He thought my meeting you would help me decide what to do."

Emily said, "We have known the Nasons for many years. I am happy Bob suggested you talk to us. Bob and Johnny were both such good boys and such good friends."

Sarah said, "Thank you for seeing me. I have a lot to decide. Honestly, I don't see how I can raise the baby. I live with my widowed mother who gets by on a small pension. She would not be capable of taking care of the baby while I work and I simply do not make enough at my job to afford child care. I'm faced with an abortion or giving the baby up for adoption."

Fred said brusquely, "Well young lady, this is none of our concern. You got yourself into this situation so now figure your way out of it."

Sarah stood up preparing to leave.

"Yes, you're right and I did not come here to dump my problem on you. I just wanted to meet Johnny's parents and I am glad I did. Thank you very much for seeing me."

Fred opened the front door.

Emily interrupted, "Just a minute here, Fred. This is our grandchild we are talking about."

"What do you mean grandchild?"

"Fred, this is Johnny's child too. Sarah, please sit down. I want to think about this a little. Fred, Johnny was our only child. He is gone. I do not like the idea of his child being aborted or given away."

"Emily for God's sake, what are you thinking?"

"I will tell you what I am thinking! I am going to the kitchen and make a pot of coffee to go along with some of that chocolate cake I baked this morning."

Emily got up, took Sarah by the hand and said, "Come with me dear. I think we have more to talk about. Come along to the kitchen Fred. Let's sit at the kitchen table."

Fred said, "For God's sake Emily, what kind of a pow-wow are you planning?"

"Never mind, we need to talk."

Emily got the coffee brewing and set out a large piece of chocolate cake for each of them.

Over cake and coffee, Emily took command. "Now Sarah, tell us about your family."

"Well, my mother is all the family I have. I was an only child. My Dad worked for the Hinckley and Northern Lumber Company until they went out of business many years ago. He bought one of their small company houses. Dad passed away several years ago and Mom and I still live in the house. Mom worked at the hardware store in Hinckley for several years but they closed up too so now she gets by on Social Security. I help out, too, as much as I can."

Emily said, "I see. I would like to meet your mother."

Fred piped up, "Emily, just what is this all about?"

"Well Fred, this is what it is all about. We lost our only child to a tragic accident. We have no close relatives other than your parents. This young woman is carrying our grandchild and has to make a decision as to what to do about it. I do not want to lose our grandchild, Fred, and I hope you just might feel the same way. From what we have heard so far she comes from a hard working respectable family that we would be proud to be associated with. Sarah, please don't be embarrassed by my thinking out loud comments. You see, Fred and I were married at a young age. We are still young enough to care for a baby. There are two empty bedrooms right down at the end of that hall and frankly, Fred, I have been thinking about talking to you about adopting a child

"What! This is all news to me! But I admit I have been a little lonely without Johnny."

"You see Sarah, we understand about losing a job and the stresses of not having enough money. Fred had a good job here until his company developed problems and eliminated his position. We moved to Chicago and worked at one of the branches. Now the firm has been purchased by another company and Fred has been given a promotion back here in Minneapolis. We feel we are back on solid ground again."

Sarah smiled. "I'm happy for you."

"Now, Sarah and Fred, hear me. I would like to meet Sarah's mother and discuss this with her and if agreeable with all, I would like very much to give consideration to our raising the child at least until such time as Sarah might desire and be able to take the responsibility herself."

Sarah's eyes filled with tears of hope. Fred scratched his chin and nodded.

"Sarah, when it comes near your time to have the baby, you could move in here with Fred and me and stay as long as you like. We would have to work out a number of details but that would be the general plan."

Sarah wiped tears from her face. "I just don't know that to say. It all sounds too good to be true."

Emily hugged Sarah, "It will all work out. We will help you through this."

Fred put an arm around Sarah and quickly wiped his own eyes.

Sarah returned home and, difficult as it was, she explained everything to her mother.

She called Bob who was elated to hear the outcome of Sarah's visit. He knew Johnny's child would survive and bring happiness to Sarah and the Edwards as well.

Bob's New Life

BOB AWOKE TO THE sound of a loud train whistle. He had stayed at a motel not too far from a railroad line. He got up, showered and dressed. He walked out into the bright early morning sunshine and over to the restaurant a short way from the motel.

Refreshed and hungry he ordered a full country breakfast of bacon and eggs with hash browns. His stomach felt good for a change after the large breakfast. While he was having his second cup of coffee, he overheard a couple of fellows at the next table discussing a successful morning of fishing on a nearby stream. Bob had not been fishing for a long time and the idea really appealed to him after hearing of their success.

Bob introduced himself to the fishermen and inquired as to where he might go if he decided to try his luck. The fellows were very friendly and gave him directions. He did have some fishing equipment in the trunk of his car and decided to give it a try. He went to the stream and in no time at all had caught two nice trout.

He worked his way up the stream and came to a railroad bridge. He climbed the bank to cross over to the other side of the bridge and noticed a vehicle coming down the tracks. The vehicle pulled up to him and stopped. To his surprise the occupants were the two fellows from the restaurant.

They struck up an immediate conversation about the fishing and about Bob. Jim Nichols and Dave Dawson were making a track inspection driving their truck over the line. Jim asked Bob where he was from and they all got acquainted. They asked what he was going to do with the trout. They told Bob the owner of the restaurant would probably fry them up and give them to him for his supper if he wanted. They told him everyone around there was pretty friendly and helpful.

Bob thanked them and added, "Incidentally, I noticed there is a support timber under the bridge which has shifted and should be corrected. It appears the water has washed away some of the gravel around the concrete footing and left it unsupported. You might want to take a look at it."

Jim said, "We sure will. Thanks a lot. We ought to get you hired on as a bridge inspector."

"I have been thinking of looking for work. Who do I see?"

"You just stop in at the engineering office in town. We do need help," said Dave.

And so it was that Bob was hired on as a chainman to accompany one of the surveyors. He found a small apartment and settled in at Duluth. With his knowledge of engineering, he was a great help to the railroad.

⚔ Visions ⚔

Bob continued to experience visions of Betty. There were times he was sure he could feel her presence. He would sometimes wake up during the night thinking he had heard her voice. It was sometimes comforting and sometimes alarming. It was beginning to cause him to become confused and depressed. As long as he was busy with his fellow employees, he was fine, but when alone and particularly at night he encountered the experiences.

After a Sunday morning mass conducted by Father Tim O'Brian, an elderly parish priest, Bob went to the rectory and asked the old man if he could sit with him and discuss a problem he was experiencing. The priest invited him in to his study.

"Well, young man what is it you wish to discuss?"

"Father, it is a rather long story but basically I have been experiencing visions of my former girl friend who died in a tragic accident and I am not sure where to start."

"I've discovered that the best place to start is at the beginning. However, young man, I happen to know a bit about that subject and best we be properly prepared. Therefore, let us first share a small glass of wine and then go down to the church basement and partake of a fine chicken dinner our social committee has prepared. We will then return and discuss your situation. You will be attending the dinner as my guest and I will be introducing you to a few of our people."

"I thank you very much father however I don't want to put you to a lot of trouble."

"You are not trouble, young man. I will be overjoyed if I can help you."

They have a glass of wine and proceed to the church basement joining the group who are enjoying the wonderful chicken dinner.

At the dinner, several of the young ladies greeted father as they served more food and drink. With a twinkle in his eye, the old Irish priest made it a point to introduce each of them to "his friend" Bob Nason. After the dinner, he sought out Ellen Riley, a tall girl, vivacious, with dark hair and a pretty smile who was the chairperson of the social committee.

"Ellen, I would like you to meet my friend, Bob Nason. Bob is new in town and I think might make a good addition to your committee if you can use the help."

"I am very happy to meet you, Bob, and yes, we can certainly use more help. If you are available please join us at our next meeting at the rectory at seven on Tuesday evening."

"Thank you for the invitation. I will try to be there," said Bob.

Father O'Brian and Bob returned to the rectory. "Alright Bob, tell me your story. Don't spare the details. I am a good listener."

Bob proceeded to relate the story of his life to the old priest. He told about his friends, their tragic deaths, his love for Betty and the visions and sensing he has been experiencing. He told about his bouts with depression and his desire to get his life back on track.

"Well, Bob, what you are experiencing is not at all unusual. In most people it lasts only a day few days. One of the most common feelings is the sense of presence. You have the feeling that your loved one is near even though you cannot see them or hear them. Some people say they hear the voice of the departed person or even feel the touch, a pat even a kiss or hug. Sometimes it is a smell or fragrance. Some people see visions in a variety of forms. We have even heard of some people having an out-of-body experience while sleeping where they feel they leave their body and visit their loved one at whatever place they feel their loved one happens to be. Bob, although there have been studies we simply do not understand this phenomenon. It occurs to many different people in many different ways and for different periods of time. I am going to give you a book which will provide you with a great deal of information on the subject. I would like you to read the book and then return so we can delve into your particular situation further. I want to assure you of one thing. Your spiritual experiences will pass. How long it will take depends on what action you take. Reading this book will be a big initial step. One other step I would highly recommend is that you attend the social committee meeting on Tuesday. Become acquainted with that group of young people and become involved with their effort. Without providing a name I will tell you at least one of those individuals has gone through the same experience you are having. You are starting a new life Bob. Cultivate new friends and new activities and your old pain and sorrow will pass. Stop in and see me in two weeks or as soon as you have finished the book."

"Thank you very much, Father, I will certainly be back."

Bob attended the Social Committee meeting and met a nice group of people. There were a few young couples and several singles. All seemed energetic and interesting. He got to see Ellen Riley in action. She introduced Bob to the group and they all seemed pleased to have him join. The purpose of this meeting was to plan for a benefit dance. They decided on a location, an orchestra and all the details necessary for the event. Ellen conducted an efficient meeting assigning tasks to various members as necessary to get the details handled.

Bob was impressed with the group and particularly with Ellen. Refreshments were served at the conclusion of the meeting so it turned into a friendly social get-together.

Bob was having a sleepless night. He tossed and turned thinking about his old friends and particularly about Betty. It was well after two a.m. before he finally fell asleep. He had troubled dreams and then the vision came. He saw Betty sitting on the end of his bed in a white flowing mesh dress. She smiled at him but did not speak. A cloud formed around her and filled the entire room. He could smell her perfume. He reached out to touch her but couldn't quite reach her. He called to her but she did not answer. Far in the background he could faintly see Johnny and then Shirley. Farther still he could just make out Bev. She seemed to be crying.

Bob was overcome with grief. He finally awoke calling out and crying. He was perspiring profusely and completely confused. He got up, showered and dressed. It was almost six a.m. He decided he had to see Father O'Brian so he went to the church and attended the early morning mass.

"Good Morning, Father Tim. I need to talk to you. I have had a terrible night. The vision came back stronger than ever. I'm afraid it is getting the best of me. I do not know how to handle this."

"Well, my son, come to the rectory at seven this evening. There is someone I would like you to meet. I think he might be able to help."

"Okay Father, I will be here. I must do something or I will lose my mind."

Bob went to work at the engineering office and returned to the rectory in the evening.

"Good evening, Bob, I would like you to meet Doctor Charles Fairchild. He is a member of our parish and helps me with difficult problems such as yours."

"Hello, Doctor. I hope you can help me."

"I am happy to meet you, Bob. Let's see what we can do."

The three went into Father O'Brian's study. Doctor Fairchild asked Bob to lie on a long couch in the room and tell him all about himself. Bob told the doctor about his friends and all that had happened. He told about Betty and the visions he was having. He told about his experience the night before. The doctor listened carefully and asked many very pointed questions about the circumstances in Bob's life.

"Bob, I am a psychiatrist. I would like your permission to hypnotize you. There will be no ill effects and it is possible we may be able to help you."

"Go ahead, Doctor, I am willing to try anything."

"Have you ever been hypnotized before?"

"No."

"Good. Alright, just relax."

The doctor had a small device in his pocket which he plugged into an outlet. It made a very small humming sound. He then took out his pocket watch, swung it back and forth in front of Bob's face and asked Bob to concentrate on the watch. He talked to Bob in a quiet voice until he was sure Bob was in a hypnotic state. The doctor again questioned Bob about his relationship with Betty and about any feelings of guilt Bob might be harboring concerning the deaths of his friends. He questioned Bob about any concerns he had in connection with the use of the explosives and the destruction of the cabin.

He explained to Bob that is was now time to eliminate all concerns he might have in connection with these events. He repeated in a number of ways that Bob should rid his mind of all negative thoughts related to these incidents. He told Bob he must free himself of thoughts of his relationship with Betty. He must realize Betty has gone to a different happy place and will never return and that Betty would want Bob to go on with his own life without her.

It was a lengthy session with Bob responding positively to the suggestions of the doctor. Finally the doctor instructed Bob to awaken. Bob felt different, refreshed with some strange sense of relief. He thanked the doctor and Father Tim.

"Bob, if you continue to experience a problem, be sure to let me know and we will try again."

"I certainly will and thank you very much again."

⚔ The Dance ⚔

I T WAS SATURDAY NIGHT and the band was hot. The hall was full as the parish dance got under way. There was old time and modern music so there was fun for the old and young alike. Bob was having a good time dancing with the ladies of the Social Committee and particularly Ellen Riley. She and Bob seemed to be developing a good relationship. There were several other lads who had their eyes on Ellen and she was kept busy.

Soft drinks were available and as the evening progressed it appeared a few of the guys were secretly carrying their own flasks of hard liquor. Apparently, they would slip into the men's room for a drink without being seen. Their actions however betrayed their secrecy.

One of the boys, Marty French, had imbibed a little too much and became rowdy. He had at one time attempted, unsuccessfully, to date Ellen. He tried to cut in while Bob was dancing with her. When it appeared she preferred to finish the dance with Bob, Marty took a big swing and struck a heavy blow to Bob's jaw.

Marty was big, and the punch knocked the unsuspecting Bob to the floor. Marty was hustled out of the hall by a couple of bouncers and taken to the police station where he was booked for assault and battery. Bob was taken to the hospital accompanied by Ellen. He was found to have a badly bruised face, cut mouth and lip. He was treated and released. The dance continued although a bit subdued for a while. The incident brought Bob and Ellen even closer together.

Some time later, Bob and Ellen were out for a dinner date and a movie. Bob asked her about Marty French.

"We were in high school together. He was a grade ahead of me. Marty was an excellent student and, as a matter of fact, was president of the senior class. He was a nice guy and well liked."

"After he graduated from high school, he went to work for a railroad as a clerk in the yard office. When they needed an extra brakeman and he was available he took that work too. He seemed to like the railroad and really learned all about their operation. Sometimes, on his day off, he would take a road trip out of town just to become familiar with the line and how the work was handled."

"We went out together to a movie once in a while. Nothing serious, just as friends and sometimes out with a group. At one point, the railroad made a force reduction and Marty took a job on an ore boat. They would take on a load of ore and ship it to places like the steel mills near Chicago and elsewhere, I guess."

"Anyway, his personality really changed after he started working on the boats. He got in with some unsavory characters, started drinking and perhaps even doing drugs, I don't know.

When the boat was here and he was off duty he and his crew mates would be drinking and carousing. I no longer wanted anything to do with him."

"Then, after a while, he seemed to have a lot of spending money. He bought a new car and new clothes and was making a big impression on a few of the people in town. I don't know where he was getting the money, but I don't think he was making that much on the boats."

"I heard he was spending time around Chicago when his boat was being unloaded and also during the off season when the boats were not operating. Someone said he was also taking flying lessons. At any rate, when he was in school he was a nice young man, but he turned into a rather rowdy ruffian after he started on the boats. I have not had anything to do with him since then."

"Well, that is quite an interesting story."

"Yes, it is. I understand his parents are pretty disappointed with the way he has changed. They are very nice. I do see his mother at church once in a while."

"But now Bob, tell me about you. You are new in town and I know very little about you. What brings you here?"

"I came here from Minneapolis wanting to get a new lease on life, so to speak. I experienced some tragic events there that are influencing me in a negative manner and I thought a change of location might help me forget."

"That sounds pretty serious. Can you tell me about it?"

"Ellen, I will tell you, however please keep this completely to yourself. Some of it is very sad and some is painful. Perhaps it might be helpful if I do confide this in you, but I will rely on you to keep it confidential. It is a long story."

Bob told his story about his friends Johnny, Shirley and Betty. He told about their tragic endings and the sadness of it all, about Sarah and the pregnancy and eventually about the visions he was experiencing and unable to control.

"Oh my God, Bob, my mother had a problem with visions after my father passed away. She is fine now but it was a difficult time for her. Father Tim helped her a great deal. I suggest you talk to him."

"Frankly, Ellen, I did meet with him and also in the company of Dr. Charles Fairchild. I am hoping it will work out. I do understand the phenomenon is not unusual, but it sure can take over your mind."

"Believe me, Bob, I know something about the subject. It will pass and you will be fine. What you need is a good friend to confide in. I will try to be that friend if you will let me."

"Thank you so much Ellen. I do appreciate it. Now it's your turn. What is your story? I know very little about you except you come highly recommended by Father O'Brian."

"Oh, there is not much to tell about me. After high school I enrolled at the university and am studying to become a pharmacist. I still have a year to go. My dad passed away two years ago. I work part time at a drug store. I live with my mother. We both try and do a little volunteer work as time permits. Mom teaches English at the "U". Enough about me. It is not too late; how about taking a little drive up to Enger Park and the Tower. You will get a beautiful view of the city and the lake from there."

They drove up to the park. Bob opened the car door for Ellen.

"Wow, what a view! This is beautiful. Look, I think I can see a ship coming in over the horizon."

"Yes, it could be an empty ore carrier or perhaps a ship coming in for a load of grain at one of the elevators. We see ships from many countries come in for grain."

After spending an hour at the park and becoming better acquainted it was time to call it a night. It was obvious their friendship was growing rapidly.

Bob had his arm around her on the ride home as they sat close and he gave her a gentle kiss when he dropped her off at her door.

The Twin Port Cities of Duluth/Superior were served by several railroads. Bob had taken a job with the Burlington Northern but became familiar with all of the others as the engineering department performed work on connections and track changes with the other lines from time to time. He enjoyed the work and was not long before he was promoted to Assistant Engineer.

⚞ Marty Returns ⚟

MARTY FRENCH WAS BACK in town. He made the rounds calling on his old friends at the yard offices of the Burlington Northern, DMIR and Soo Line railroads. He liked to drive in with his new car, hand out a few cigars and look over the train consists to see what was moving those days. He was always careful not to stop in if he had been drinking. He frequently gave the impression he might return to work for the railroad if conditions were right. In the meantime, he wanted to keep his friends and keep abreast of what was going on.

The friends didn't mind his stopping in and sometimes listened to his interesting stories of some of the great times he had in Chicago or other places he had visited. He was particularly friendly with Rick Baxter, one of the evening clerks at the Burlington Northern who had access to information on their entire system. He was always interested in seeing what was moving and where.

As he looked over the train lists, one load in particular caught his eye. CP 234789 whiskey for New Orleans, LA. It was routed via Burlington Northern to Superior, Soo Line to Chicago and Illinois Central beyond.

While Rick went to the bathroom, Marty stuffed a few copies of blank waybill forms into an inside pocket of his jacket. He then jotted down the information from the waybill for the car of whiskey and stuffed that into his pocket too. Being well-versed on the operation, he was able to figure out the approximate time the car would be placed on the interchange track to the Soo Line. Completing his visit with Rick, he gave him a handful of cigars and left.

Marty went over to a restaurant, took a booth in a far corner ordered some pie and perused a copy of the daily newspaper. After the waitress delivered his order, he pulled out a blank waybill form from his pocket and using a marking pencil he proceeded to fill it out with the information he had noted on the original waybill but with a stop off in Chicago.

The stop-off waybill had a space for special instructions so he wrote (Notify Citywide Storage and Transfer at 609 777 8444). That phone number was a pay phone in Blacky Barzono's pool hall in Cicero. When the phone rang, an extension buzzed in Tony Pestilano's upstairs back office.

After completing the stop-off waybill, he tucked it in his pocket and left. He drove to the Radisson Hotel, went to a public phone booth and called Chicago.

"Hi Tony, this is Marty. How ya doin?"

"Couldn't be better. How you doin?"

"Tip Top, Tony. How would you like to do a little business?"

"What you got?"

"How about a carload of Canadian booze. Does that sound appealing?"

"A whole carload?"

"Yes. It is headed for New Orleans but I think I can divert it to you if you can handle it. If you are not interested I got another connection farther south."

"Sounds like you are playing me against another guy Marty. I don't like that."

"Just business Tony, you know that."

"When can you get it here?"

"Couple days."

"Yeah, I can handle it. How much you asking?"

"Tony, you know it's got to be good stuff, probably Crown Royal."

"So - how much you want?"

"I'll take five G's, Tony."

"Are you going to deliver it?"

"No, Tony, you will have to unload it and haul it from track."

"So I take all the chances?"

"Ya. You will be notified when it arrives in town. You decide where you want the car spotted and you take it from there."

"I see. I will give you three G's."

"Not enough, Tony. I am taking a big risk here and I have to pay other people to get the job done."

"Okay, let's split the difference, make it four G's."

"Okay Tony, you wire me the four G's in advance today."

"Oh no, the offer is four G's cash in my office after I get the goods."

"You are a tough guy to deal with Tony, but you have a deal. I will come down for the money after you unload the goods. I will have a guy call you when it hits town."

Marty hung up and called another number in Chicago.

"Hello Georgio, this is Marty. How have you been?"

"Been good, Marty. How are you doing? Haven't heard from you for a while."

"Ya, I know. I haven't been down to Chicago for a while. Busy, busy, busy you know."

"Me, too. This place is a rat race sometimes."

Georgio was the chief clerk in the Soo Line railroad yard office in Chicago. He was in charge of all the clerical operations in the office.

"I don't want to keep you, Georgio, but maybe we can do a little business. I'm working on this shipment coming out of Canada headed for New Orleans. I'm planning on a stop off in Chicago. I would like to have you watch for the car and handle the paper work yourself. The regular waybill is clean but there will be a stop-off waybill with special instructions to call a guy when it arrives at your place. He will tell you where he wants it spotted for unloading. You have it spotted and after he unloads, you tear up the stop- off billing and send the car on its way just as if it never stopped."

"Okay, I get the picture. Who are we dealing with here?"

"It's our old friend Tony Pestilano. You remember him. We had some good times down there."

"So this takes especially careful handling, right?"

"You got it, Georgio. You will have to take care of the whole thing yourself."

"I can handle it, Marty, of course it will cost you."

"I know and I am going to make it well worth your while. I will be coming down there to collect from Tony right after the deal is done. You and Tony and I will go out and have a little party, maybe with the girls at Gigi's."

"Sounds good. What's the car number and when will it be here."

"It is CP 234789 and it will be transferred from the Burlington to the Soo Line at Superior this afternoon. I am working on the paperwork right now. It should arrive at Schiller sometime tomorrow afternoon. You can watch the train consists on the departure lists out of Shops Yard."

"Okay Marty, we have a deal."

Marty drove over to "The Shack" restaurant for lunch.

"Hi beautiful, how is my favorite waitress today?"

"Just fine, as usual. How is my favorite customer?"

"Great, Gladys. How about a nice steak sandwich and a manhattan?"

"Coming right up, handsome."

Gladys brings over the manhattan.

"Two extra cherries just for you, my friend. And the sandwich will be up shortly."

"You don't look too busy right now. Do you have time to sit down and have a drink with me?"

"Not while I am on duty, Marty. I don't want to get fired."

"Well, when will you be off duty?"

"It is slow today so I will only work until after the lunch hour. I will be out at two thirty."

"How about getting together after that? We could take a little ride up around the north shore."

"Oh, I don't think so, Marty, but thanks for asking."

"Oh, come on. I have a brand new Caddy, you know."

"Now, Marty, you know I'm married to a nice guy and I don't cheat on my Eddie."

"Is Eddie out of town again?"

"Yes, he and that new guy are inspecting some bridges up north and won't be back until tomorrow, I guess."

"Well, Gladys, it's not like you would be cheating. We will just take a ride up around the lake a ways and maybe stop for dinner."

"So you have a new Cadillac again, huh?"

"Yup, rides like a baby buggy."

Marty takes a sip of his manhattan and winks at Gladys.

"Do you know who the guy from the engineering department is?"

"Not really. I guess it is some new guy by the name of Bob something or other."

"I see. Ya, I think I have heard of him."

"I see your sandwich is ready. I will bring it right over."

Gladys brings the sandwich.

"Thanks. Incidentally I have to say you look fantastic in that new uniform."

"Oh crap, I don't like them. Too drafty -- these short skirts and low cut blouses are almost embarrassing. And Eddie doesn't like me wearing it."

"Well, you know sex sells and with your figure I certainly wouldn't be embarrassed."

"You think so?"

"I know so. You have great legs."

"Now you are making me blush."

"So - a little blushing never hurt a girl."

"You are such a tease."

"Listen Gladys, I have some things I have to do this afternoon but how would it be if I pick you up about six o'clock. We will take a ride up around the lake and maybe have dinner at that little out of the way place called The Hideout."

"That does sound like fun."

"Sure it would be and we would be home early."

"Well, okay Marty, but no funny business."

"I'll pick you up about six."

Gladys left to attend to another customer. Marty finished his lunch, slapped down a ten dollar tip and waved to Gladys as he went out the door.

Marty drove over to Stinson yard to visit with the afternoon chief yard clerk. He walked in and dropped a carton of cigarettes on Luke Larson's desk.

"Hi, Luke. How is it going? Are you doing any business?"

"Freight is moving pretty good. When are you coming back to work? I heard they could use you over at the BN."

"Well, I'll see. Maybe I could catch a little relief work before the boats start again."

"What are you doing with all your spare time?"

"Just living the good life. I saved my money from working on the boats and now I'm spending a little. I am taking flying lessons and took my first solo flight last week. I am going to Chicago early next week for a few days."

"What a life. Where are you taking flying lessons?"

"It is a guy out at Solon Springs that has his own plane. As soon as I am good enough I will be able to rent the plane from him quite reasonably."

"Has the BN delivered to the transfer yet?"

"No, they should be over there in about an hour."

"I hear you have a new trainmaster over here."

"Ya, and the cockroach has his nose into everything. He even comes down here in the middle of the night to check on things. He would like to figure out a way to cut off the ten thirty switch engine."

"I guess that's his job. That's what he gets paid for."

"I know, but the guys don't like him looking over their shoulder all the time."

"Well, I gotta go, Luke. Take care. See ya next time."

Marty left and drove down to South Superior and went to the Interchange Bar.

He took a stool at the end of the bar nearest the window. From there he was able to see the Burlington Northern switch engine pulling by to deliver cars to the Soo Line interchange track.

"Well, well! The rabble-rouser is back in town. What brings you here?"

"Why, what do you mean, Jeannie, calling a nice, quiet, mild-mannered fellow like me a rabble-rouser?"

"Mild-mannered my ass! It cost me five hundred bucks to patch this place up the last time you and your damn drunken boat buddies were in here brawling."

"Now, Jeannie we weren't the ones who started that fight. It was those damn stump-jumping, pulp-cutting relatives of yours."

"Well, my poor husband had a heart attack not long after that episode. He couldn't handle a fracas like that."

"Sorry about that, Jeannie. You running the place yourself now?"

"Yes and no. I am running it but I got a three hundred pound guy that used to be a boxer living upstairs and helping me out evenings. Are you going to buy something or are you just going to sit around and yap?"

"I intended to buy something, but you kept interrupting me with all those insults. Give me a nickel beer."

"Nickel beer! This ain't 1930 you know."

"I would order a martini but I don't suppose you sell them in a crummy place like this."

"Listen, buster, I can make a martini that will knock your socks off."

"Okay, let me try one and I want a twist of lemon and two olives."

"Okay, I will mix it up and if you fall off the barstool I will simply have my big friend from upstairs toss you into the dumpster out back."

"Jeannie, you are a true friend. I am going to have to stop in here more often just to prove what a nice fellow I am."

"You do that. Now here is your martini, tell me how you like it."

Marty passed the drink under his nose, breathed in the aroma and took a sip.

"Say girl, I think I have to eat crow. This is a great martini. It tastes like Fleischmann's Gin but what kind of vermouth is it?"

"That is my secret. You know I used to be a bartender at the Ritz Hotel in Chicago years ago."

"No kidding. I bet you were great."

"Yup, I wasn't bad looking back in those days but I pissed off a mafia guy with my sharp tongue and it turned out he owned the place. After that, I couldn't get a job anywhere in Chicago, so we moved up here."

"Well, see there -- now you can use your sharp tongue to your heart's content."

"You're damn right. I don't take crap from any of the clowns that come in here."

Marty looked out the window and could see the BN transfer pulling by.

"Jeannie, I would like another one of these wonderful martinis but it is a little early in the day. I will certainly be back another time for another one. You have a good day."

He tucked a ten dollar bill in her bra and left.

Marty drove around the wooded area beyond the transfer and watched while the BN made their delivery and picked up the cars they would take back to the BN yard.

When they left, he walked through the woods to the little shanty at the track. Just inside the door was a metal box fastened with two locks. It could be opened with either a BN switch key or a Soo Line key. It was for use by the crews to exchange the waybills that accompanied the cars being interchanged.

Marty unlocked the box with his key, removed the waybills. He found the waybill for the load of whiskey. He had brought a small stapler with him and attached the stop-over waybill which he had prepared, to the regular waybill covering the through movement. He placed the entire bundle back in the box and re-locked it.

Marty whistled as he walked back to his car. He was feeling great. He would be heading to Chicago for the payoff in a couple of days.

Marty drove up to Gladys' house and rang the bell. She answered promptly and was all dressed to go.

"Hey, girl, you clean up real good. That is a pretty fancy outfit."

"Just for you, Marty. Can't drive around in a fancy car with a fancy guy unless you have a fancy outfit."

"Okay, babe, let's head out around the north shore. We can enjoy the view at a couple of the outlooks and then stop at the Hideout."

"Sounds good to me. Wow! This is a fancy car."

Gladys sat close to Marty and he put his arm around her as he drove with one hand. The scenery was beautiful. They stopped at a wayside outlook point and watched a couple deer scamper along the lakeshore.

⚔ Back at Stinson Yard ⚔

"Hey, Baxter, this is Luke over at Stinson. The switch crew just brought your drag over from the interchange and I have a question about one of the cars."

"What do you need, Luke?"

"You sent over a car of whiskey with a stop-over in Chicago but there is no waybill number and no connection shown on the waybill. Will you check your train lists and give me the information?"

"Sure, what is the car number?"

"CP 234789 Whiskey out of Canada."

"Let me see. Just a minute I will see what I can find."

"Okay, I will hang on."

"Hey, Luke, that car doesn't show as a stop-over on my lists."

"That's funny. It is a handwritten stop-over waybill and I see it also doesn't indicate if the stop-over is prepaid or not."

"Well Bax, this doesn't look right."

"I agree. We have nothing here to indicate it is to stop-over anywhere."

"Okay, I am going to hold the car right here until we can get this straightened out. I will try and reach the shipper and see what he has to say."

"Good idea. Let me know what you find out."

"Okay. Bye, Bax."

Luke called telephone directory information and obtained a phone number for the shipper, Alberta Distillers, Calgary, Alberta, Canada. He was able to reach their switchboard and they directed his call to their shipping department. It was after working hours, but there was a billing clerk in the office. The clerk checked their records and there was no indication of a stop-over on the car. He called their traffic manager at his home who confirmed the fact and suggested something was awry.

He requested that Luke hold the car and inform the local office of the FBI. He would contact the local freight agent first thing in the morning and check the records at all locations on the line that could have added the stop-over instructions.

Luke made a record of all of his conversations. He instructed the switch crew to spot the car on a track right near the yard office where it could be watched. He also called the Duluth branch office of the FBI and explained the situation. Somebody was interfering with interstate commerce.

An FBI agent arrived at Stinson Yard in about an hour. Luke showed him the waybills and his notes. He took the stop-over waybill and went over to the Burlington yard office and discussed it with Rick Baxter. The FBI agent was immediately suspicious that someone at the BN office was responsible. He questioned Rick thoroughly. Rick denied having anything to do with it.

He did remember that Marty French had been in the office visiting earlier that day. They checked the supply of waybills in the office and found the form number and printer of the supply on hand was identical to the form of the stop-over waybill.

Marty had once worked in the office, so they looked back in the files to see if they could find any of Marty's handwriting. They found some old yard lists which had been written by Marty. The FBI agent felt there were definite similarities and would be following up with Mr. Martin French the following day.

⚔ At The Hideout ⚔

MARTY AND GLADYS WERE having a good time with lots of laughs as they arrived at The Hideout. The place lived up to its name. In addition to the regular bar and dining room area, it had a wing for strict privacy if desired.

A hallway extended the length of the wing with enclosed cubicles on each side of the hallway. A couple could enter the cubicle, close the door and dine in complete privacy. As soon as they were seated, they could press a button on the wall which turned on a light at the bar, signaling that they desired service. The bartender could respond over a small speaker and they could place their order with him. It would then be delivered through a small door in the wall accompanied by a menu. If dinner was desired it could be ordered and delivered in the same manner.

Marty and Gladys each ordered a martini and a steak. They could faintly hear a band at the other end of the building but decided not to dance. Under the circumstances, it was best they stay out of sight in the privacy of the cubicle.

Gladys' husband Eddie, and Bob finished their bridge inspection earlier than anticipated. Even though it would be late, they decided they would rather drive home than stay out another night. They stopped to eat at a little restaurant, gassed up the truck and headed for home.

Eddie and Bob had become good friends and frequently discussed their personal lives with each other. Bob confided about the problem he had been having with the visions of Betty. Eddie confided he was not happy with Gladys working at "The Shack" however it did give her something to do when he spent so much time out of town.

They discussed a lot of the ups and downs in their lives. Eddie was proud of the work he had done on his house. He lived part way up a hill but his view of the lake had been partially blocked by the house next door, so he had built an extension out the south side and a patio beyond. The first floor was a sun room and above that was an open porch with a railing. He installed a doorway from the upstairs hallway to the porch. The bedrooms were on the second floor so he could slip out of bed and sit out in the air if he wished during the night.

From both the sun room and the porch they had a clear view of Lake Superior. He loved to sit on the porch and watch the activity in the harbor. He could watch the activity at the grain elevators and in the rail yards.

The patio just out from the sun porch led to a flower garden which Gladys tended religiously. He had built a little fountain waterfall over rocks at one end. There were bird feeders and, of course, it was always a problem to keep the squirrels from stealing the bird seed.

Eddie and Gladys were happy there. She was a good wife. They had raised two daughters who were now grown and married. Gladys had raised them well. He was very proud of them. Gladys would like to travel and get out more but it was difficult with Eddie's demanding job.

He wasn't one who cared about going out to eat or movies and such. Gladys missed that, but she didn't complain much. He felt guilty about not entertaining her more.

Bob told Eddie he had been seeing Ellen Riley some. He and Ellen had become good friends since he came to Duluth, but it was nothing serious. He enjoyed spending time with her but it didn't seem to get too romantic. They went on several dates, exchanged their life stories, kissed after parking at the lake, etc.

Ellen was serious about her studies and would certainly make a fine pharmacist some day.

The time was passing quickly and they would be home in a few hours.

⚔ Enjoying Dinner ⚔

MARTY AND GLADYS WERE enjoying a great dinner and having a good time at The Hideout. Marty had a lot of jokes and stories. He could be a real charmer with the ladies. Eventually, they finished their dinner, had an after dinner drink and headed back to town. Gladys took her shoes off, curled up tight to Marty with her head on his shoulder as he drove with an arm around her.

"This is so nice Marty. It is so much fun being with you."

"Well, Gladys, it is fun to be with you too. This has been a great evening. We should do this more often."

"Oh Marty, I would like that."

"Maybe I could take you to Chicago with me sometime."

"Oh, I don't know how I could get away with that. Eddie is a very understanding guy but I'm sure he wouldn't put up with that. He will be plenty wild if he finds out I went out to dinner with you."

They soon arrived at Gladys' house and parked in the driveway. The car was somewhat hidden by the trees along the drive.

"Would you like to come in for some apple pie and coffee?"

"That would be great. Did you bake it yourself?"

"Oh yes, it's my mother's recipe. I baked it fresh this morning."

"Okay, I'm all for apple pie and whatever goes with it."

They went to the kitchen and Marty gave her a hug and a kiss on the cheek while she prepared the coffee. She turned to face him and returned a big hug. They held it and she kissed him again, full on the lips. Backing away, she hesitated a moment and then dished out the pie, adding whipping cream to each piece. As soon as the coffee was ready she filled the cups. They both sat at the same side of the table having their dessert.

Marty finished and put one arm around her and with the other found his way inside her blouse and fondled her breasts. She objected only mildly, so he continued.

One thing followed another and in a short while they were in the bedroom. As they undressed, Gladys saw a gun strapped to Marty's leg.

"A gun? Marty, is that a gun?"

"Don't worry, sweetie. It won't hurt you. All my Chicago friends carry a gun like that. It is just some protection you need in the big city."

"I don't know Marty -- it frightens me."

"Don't worry, Gladys; it is nothing. I will just lay it here on top of my shoe."

"I don't know, Marty, it looks dangerous, but exciting!"

In a moment the lights were out and they were engaged in wild sex. Soon after, they were both asleep.

It was almost midnight when Bob and Eddie arrived in town. Bob drove to Eddie's house to drop him off. They pulled into the driveway and saw the Cadillac parked in front of the garage.

"Looks like you have company, Eddie."

"Who the hell? Bob, I know that car. It belongs to that bastard Marty French."

Eddie reached for the shotgun hanging just behind their heads in the cab of the truck. They carried a gun for protection against bears and wolves out in some of the wilderness for work along the tracks. Bob grabbed for the gun but Eddie pulled it out of his hand.

"Hold it, Eddie. Don't get too excited. This might not be what you think."

"Let's find out. Come on."

Bob followed right behind as Eddie carefully unlocked the door, left it open and tip-toed inside. The house was dark and quiet. Eddie started up the carpeted stairway to the second floor. As he reached the top, he flipped the light switch on. When he did, he bumped the wall with the butt of the gun.

Marty was awake in a flash, grabbed his gun and jumped into the hallway. He saw Eddie with the shotgun and fired the pistol striking Eddie in the leg. Eddie fell but pulled the trigger on the shotgun as he was going down. Plaster and wood slivers fell on Marty as the shotgun blast ripped into the ceiling just above his head. He ran out the door and onto the porch, jumped up on a chaise lounge and over the railing toward the ground. His right foot hit the railing as he jumped over and tripped him as he fell head first onto the patio below.

Bob grabbed the gun from Eddie and raced to the porch. A motion light had turned on and Bob saw Marty naked, unconscious with his head bleeding profusely, sprawled on the patio below.

Gladys was screaming as she ran naked into the hall. Bob yelled at her to call 911. Obeying, she ran to the phone in the bedroom and dialed. Bob ran to the bathroom, got a towel and wrapped it around Eddie's bleeding leg. He then told Gladys to put some clothes on.

The police and an ambulance arrived in minutes. Bob told Gladys to hold the towel on Eddie as he ran downstairs to direct them to Marty. It was too late. His skull was cracked open as he lay in a pool of his own blood.

The police called for the coroner and the body was taken to the morgue. Meanwhile, the paramedics tended to Eddie. They stopped his bleeding and rushed him to the hospital.

Gladys and Bob stayed behind to explain quickly to the police what had happened before they, too, rushed to the hospital.

When they arrived, Eddie was in the emergency room. Surgeons were preparing to remove the slug from his leg. He was pale and had lost a lot of blood. Gladys rushed to him, threw her arms around him and sobbed. She was in anguish and overwhelmed with sorrow.

Attendants forced her away to the waiting room so they could work on Eddie. He needed blood and they were low on supply for his type. Bob had them check him and found his blood type matched, so they were able to make a quick direct transfer from Bob to Eddie.

Gladys was sobbing and saying she wanted to die. She had to be sedated. Eddie's wounds were cleaned and stitched. He was treated for shock and taken to the intensive care unit for further monitoring.

Gladys was taken to a separate room and placed under suicide watch in a bed with restraints and monitored closely. Bob was completely exhausted. There was nothing more he could do so he went home and fell into bed.

The morning news had the police report on Marty's untimely death.

The FBI agent having his morning coffee couldn't believe it. This was the man he was going to search for and question the first thing that morning!

Marty's car had been towed to the police holding lot. With the cooperation of the police department, the FBI agent obtained finger prints from the steering wheel and door handles and compared them with finger prints on the stop-over waybill. There was a good match, so there was no doubt the scheme was Marty's doings.

After confirming details with the railroads, the car was released toward its final destination. The stop-over waybill was sent to the Chicago FBI office for further follow up of those involved. There was no doubt this would lead to investigation of some of the crime element in Chicago.

Engine Wreck

THE PHONE RANG NONSTOP. Bob finally awakened from a deep sleep and answered.

"What? Where? On it's side? Burning? Okay, I am on my way."

Bob bounded out of bed, got dressed and rushed off to the dock area. A switch crew had just had a terrible accident. A bridge at the waterfront had collapsed. The locomotive was partially on its side, hanging over the water and teetering. The crew was trapped inside unable to get out because a bridge timber had fallen and blocked the doorway.

Attached to the engine was a carload of propane gas which had been punctured and was leaking. The fire department has been called and a wrecking crew was on its way. Help was needed immediately.

Bob was the first to arrive at the scene. The two occupants of the engine were waving franticly from inside the cab. The cab had twisted and buckled so the windows could not be opened. A bridge timber was wedged between the car of propane and the engine.

It appeared the engine would tumble into the deep water momentarily. Bob rushed to the hand brake wheel on the trailing end of the car of propane and turned it as tightly as he could, setting the brakes on the car. He found an iron plate beside the track and placed that in front of a wheel. He climbed up on the tank car of propane and carefully worked his way toward the teetering engine.

It was extremely dangerous. The engine and car of propane could both slide into the water at any moment. Bob got to the end of the tank car and leaped across to the engine. He lifted on the bridge timber but was unable to move it. Looking about for something to pry it with, he saw a loose plank near the top of the partially-collapsed bridge framework. He jumped back to the tank car, clambered up on top of the leaking car, and from a very precarious position, reached up and pulled down the heavy wooden plank.

It was a very dangerous thing to do but he knew the lives of those in the cab of the engine were at stake. He managed to get the plank down and over to the engine. Using the plank as a pry, he was able to move the timber enough so the two inside the engine were able to squeeze through the partially opened door. After they were out, he then laid the plank down extending it from the engine to the tank car and all three crossed to safety.

By this time a crowd had assembled and cheered as the engine crew hugged and thanked Bob for saving their lives. In the excitement, he had not noticed that one member of the crew was a woman. The two were dressed alike in overalls, jackets and caps. It was only when she hugged him and gave him a kiss did he realize it was not a man. What a surprise!

There was extreme danger of fire and explosion from the punctured and leaking tank car of propane so the crowd was quickly ordered to leave the area. The fire department took over. They misted and foamed the area and applied a large patch of a special material on the leak securing it in place with a wide belt around the entire car.

Two huge wrecking cranes were brought in along with winch-equipped caterpillars. Large cables were attached to both the engine and the heavy tank car. It was very difficult to pull them back to solid track. It took all day, but inch by inch the car and engine were pulled back and re-railed. Bob was proclaimed to be a real hero.

That evening Bob went to the hospital to visit his friend Eddie. He arrived to find Ed alone in his room and quite depressed. The wound in his leg was giving him quite a bit of pain. There was fear it might be infected.

Eddie cried when he thought about his wife in bed with that damn Marty French.

"Bob, why the hell would she do such a thing? I can't believe she would cheat on me like that. How often has she done this?"

"Eddie, I do not have the answer to those questions but I do know she loves you more than anything in the world. She is in terrible pain with guilt from it all. From what I am seeing, I really doubt that she was ever unfaithful to you other than this one time. I understand Marty was a real woman charmer. No doubt he got her to drink too much and she didn't really realize the consequences of what she was doing."

"I hate to say it Bob, but that bastard got his due. He won't be charming any more women."

"Right. There were only a few people at his funeral. I understand the FBI is checking him out and finding he was involved with a bunch of illegal stuff with some mafia guys in Chicago."

"So that is where he was getting his money from and always riding around in a new Cadillac."

"That is the way it looks. You can see how Gladys might have been impressed."

"You know Bob, I didn't take her out much and I was gone a lot so maybe she was lonely at times."

"Sure she was Eddie. I know you are a good man. I hope you find it in your heart to forgive her and still love her."

Eddie broke down crying. Bob went to the bed and put his arm around Eddie.

"I do love her, Bob, but this really tears me apart."

"I know, Ed, and she loves you too. You get some rest now and I will be back tomorrow evening."

"Thanks, Bob, you are a good friend."

Bob stopped at Gladys' room and found her asleep. She had been heavily sedated and he noted a strap attached to her wrist and the side of the bed. He walked away down the hall with a heavy heart. He felt very sorry for both Ed and Gladys.

On his way home, Bob stopped for gas, a lottery ticket and a newspaper. He smiled when he glanced at the front page photos of the train wreck. He drove past Eddie's house then up the hill and through the park.

When he got home, he called Ellen. She had seen the paper and was very excited.

"Well, hello hero! I had no idea you were so brave!"

"What do you mean?"

"Have you seen tonight's paper? You are simply amazing! I am so proud of you!"

"Gee, thanks. What did I do to deserve such praise?"

"The paper is full of pictures of you at the train wreck saving the crew from almost certain death."

"It was no more than anyone would have done."

"Well, look and behold. The word on the street is that the mayor, who was out of town today, will be looking for you. I think there might be a reward in your future."

"My reward was helping them to safety."

"Honestly, Ellen, I feel very sad tonight. I just returned from visiting Eddie. He is really depressed and Gladys is being sedated and restrained. What a terrible turn of events in their life."

"I know, Bob. When I was volunteering at the hospital today, I overheard the doctors saying that his leg is not responding to treatment. This is not for publication, but there is some possibility he might lose the leg."

"It is just a bullet wound, but it could have torn through a major blood vessel the way he was bleeding. God, I hope he doesn't lose a leg."

"I will be there again tomorrow and will see what I can find out."

"Would you also look in on Gladys? This has obviously hit her extremely hard. She must be unstable. They actually have her restrained."

"I understand she has been a wonderful wife and mother and a very fine person. As a matter of fact, she also volunteered at the hospital from time to time."

"Well, let's hope for the best. Keep me informed."

"Okay, Bob, I mean hero - good night."

"Good night, and it's just plain Bob to you Ellen. Sweet dreams."

⚔ Plaque of Honor ⚔

B OB ARRIVED AT THE engineering office at seven thirty and looked over the morning reports. The derailment had been cleared up but he would have to inspect the bridge to determine what repairs would be required. He would have to do it alone, since Ed was still in the hospital.

The rest of the office force arrived just before eight o'clock and following them were the chief engineer, the mayor, photographers and the two crew members he had saved. The chief engineer ushered them all into the conference room and summoned Bob to join them. With the entire group assembled, the mayor opened his brief case and brought out a large plaque. Bob stood between the Chief Engineer and the mayor and with the photographers snapping pictures, the mayor congratulated Bob and presented him with the plaque.

"Mr. Robert Nason, as Mayor of Duluth, Minnesota, it is indeed my great pleasure to present to you this plaque and accompanying certificate bestowing upon you the distinct honor of being declared the 'Hero of the Year." Upon all the evidence of the many individuals who witnessed your daring feat, resulting in the saving of two lives, there is no doubt whatsoever you are indeed most deserving of this honor. On behalf of the citizens of our city, your employer, and myself, I congratulate you and thank you most sincerely."

Bob was overwhelmed. Everyone present was shaking his hand and congratulating him. He was at a loss for words. The two crew members were almost in tears as they hugged him and thanked him.

It turned out they were a father, in his middle fifties and the daughter a beautiful young lady in her twenties. She wanted to become a locomotive engineer like her father so had been accompanying him as a student.

Bob finally found his voice thanked the mayor and the chief engineer. He was completely humbled by the award and somewhat embarrassed by all the attention. As the crowd cleared and the photographers left, the two crew members remained behind to talk further with Bob.

The engineer, tall and slim with dark wavy hair graying at the sides, blue eyes and a ready smile introduced himself to Bob.

"My name is John Bolton and this is my daughter Sue. I have been a locomotive engineer for many years. Sue has been fascinated by locomotives since she was a little girl and now wants to learn how to operate one. I cannot express our thanks enough for your saving our lives. It was a horrendous experience and there is no doubt in my mind that if you had not been there to remove that heavy bridge timber from the door we would not have survived. I want to thank you from the bottom of my heart."

"John, the pleasure is mine. I hope you never find yourself in a situation like that again."

Sue, tall, blond, blue eyed and beautiful said, "Bob I, too, wish to thank you so much. I cannot tell you how frightened I was. Every time that locomotive teetered I thought my life was going to be over. You saved our lives and we will be forever grateful."

"I don't know what to say. I am so happy it turned out this way," said Bob.

John said, "Bob, my wife couldn't be here with us this morning but she asked us to invite you over for dinner on Sunday. She would like to meet you. We would be honored if you would come."

"Well John, thank you. If you promise to tell her not to fuss I will be happy to join you."

Bob couldn't help but notice the pretty smile on her face as Sue said, "Bye, see you Sunday."

Bob stopped at the hospital on his way home from work. He found Ed in a wheelchair reading the evening paper. It was full of pictures and a lengthy article concerning the award having been presented to Bob. "Well Mr. Nason, it appears you are the 'Man of the Year' in this fair city."

"Oh it wasn't that big a deal Ed. They just made a big deal out of it."

"Not the way I read this. Bob, you saved those folks lives. You can be very proud of yourself."

"To be truthful Ed, I was shaking in my boots the whole time. That engine was just about ready to go into the drink. If it had gone down I guess I would have gone down with it too. That is enough about me. How are you doing?"

"Well I am in better shape today than I was yesterday. I understand an infection was spreading like wildfire but they have it stopped for now. They obtained some special medicine from the Mayo Clinic and that seems to be working. They're checking it every few hours. With the pain meds they are letting me move around in the wheelchair. The doctors scared the hell out of me when were talking about taking the leg off but I guess we are out of danger with that now."

"Well that is good news. I'm sure happy to hear that."

"A friend of yours stopped in to see me this afternoon."

"Oh, who might that have been?"

"A mighty fine looking young lady by the name of Ellen Riley."

"Yes, she is a friend and she does volunteer work here."

"You know, Bobby, I got the feeling she is more than just a friend. Could that be the case?"

"Not yet, but you never know. Oh we have gone out a few times but nothing really serious but who knows."

"She asked if I would like to go and see Gladys. Well, I wasn't sure what to do about that but I said okay. She took me down the hall and up to the next floor to Gladys' room. As mad as I am at her for what she did, I really feel sorry for her. She was lying there crying. Her arm was strapped to the bed so she couldn't leave by herself." Bob shook his head and put a hand on Eddie's shoulder.

"She is overwhelmed with sorrow and can't seem to snap out of it. Ellen rolled me into the room and up to the bed and Gladys wouldn't look at me. She just turned away and cried louder and louder. I broke down too and reached over and put my hand on hers. She pulled her hand away crying "I'm so sorry, I don't deserve you."

"Damn it, Eddie, I feel so sorry for both of you."

"You know Bob, it hurts like hell, what she did-- but I still love her."

"And I know she loves you Eddie."

"Ellen asked if it would be okay if she asked the priest, Father Tim O'Brian from her church to come and visit with Gladys. I said sure if she thought it would help. Gladys has to be brought out of this terrible frame of mind somehow."

"I know Father O'Brian. He is a wise old man. I think it would be helpful for him to talk to her."

"Ellen is going to talk to him this evening so perhaps he will stop in tomorrow."

"Well Eddie, I am certainly happy to see you doing better. I will stop in again tomorrow evening. If they get that infection cured and patch that leg up, you might be able to get out of here in a day or two."

"That would be great. Thanks for coming by. You are a friend and, oh yes, a hero."

"Get some rest, Eddie."

Eddie rolled his chair over to the window. He had a good view of the downtown area and the waterfront. He could see a ship sailing in and about to come under the lift bridge and into the harbor. It was almost dusk and lights were turning on all around the city. It was quiet in his room except for an occasional ringing of the telephone at the nurse's station down the hall.

Eddie thought about his situation. He couldn't help but wonder about his future. He wondered if his leg would heal properly so he could work again. He couldn't get Gladys off his mind. She was obviously very unstable right now. Would she be able to snap out of it? Could he love her again as he once did? Would he be able to trust her in the future?

He could see a big vast world out the window. He felt insignificant in that world but his head and heart were full and heavy in this room. Would the pain ever go away? Would he ever be the same again?

Bob returned to his apartment filled with sadness for his friends Eddie and Gladys. He didn't feel like preparing a meal for himself. He looked in his refrigerator and nothing appealed to him. He looked at the newspaper for a few minutes then picked up the phone and called Ellen.

"Wow it looks like they devoted the entire newspaper to our hero."

"Ya, they have to have something to fill the pages I guess."

"Well Bob, I am glad you are getting the recognition you deserve."

"Thanks, Ellen, that is nice of you to say. I stopped at the hospital on my way home and talked to Eddie. Sounds like his leg is going to be okay but I don't know what to think about Gladys."

"I know."

"Have you had supper yet, El? I don't feel like preparing anything. How would you like to go out for pizza or Chinese or something?"

"Does this mean you are asking me out on a date?"

"Well, I wouldn't call it an official type date but if you would prefer not to I guess I will have to be satisfied with just calling it a casual impromptu meeting or something like that. Your choice."

"Well, I am certainly not going to turn down an offer by the hero of the year. I will consider it a real date and note it as such in my diary!"

"So be it. I will pick you up in half an hour."

They decided to go to the Green Lantern for Chinese. The food was always great. The atmosphere was pleasant and they were able to find a quiet corner table.

"As long as you want to consider this an official date with the acclaimed hero of the year, would you mind joining said hero with a cocktail before dinner?"

"I most certainly would not mind as long as said hero is buying, and in which case I will have a Southern Comfort old fashioned."

"That sounds like a good choice. I think I will have one of the same."

They ordered drinks and dinner and immediately Gladys' and Eddie's situation came up.

"I suppose Eddie told you that I stopped in to see him today and took him up to see Gladys."

"Yes, he did and thanks for trying, El, but it sounded like a horrible meeting of the two today."

"You should have been there Bob. I had to cry right along with them. It was so sad. He is obviously extremely hurt and angry at what she did but still loves her and it tears him apart. And Gladys is completely overwhelmed with guilt and cries constantly."

"I understand you are going to talk to Father Tim about her."

"Yes, actually I did talk to him today. He will go over and visit with her right after the morning mass tomorrow. Maybe he can bring her out of that awful mental place she is in."

"Here are our drinks and here is a toast and congratulations to the hero of the town!"

"Well, thank you, Ellen, and here is a toast to the best looking girl in the room."

"Oh my, thank you, sir."

"What is the scuttlebutt at the hospital, Ellen? Will they be able to save Eddie's leg?"

"Oh, I am quite sure they will. I understand they removed some of the infected flesh, used some new strong antibiotic and the infection seems to be under control. They will probably stitch it up tomorrow and monitor him carefully for a few days to see if there are any flare ups in his system. I do think it is going to be okay."

"That is really good news."

"Just keep your fingers crossed."

"Well, Ellen, I hope their marriage doesn't go down the drain."

"Me, too."

"Eddie told me they have two grown daughters. They are both married and live away somewhere. As far as I know they are not aware of what is going on here. I wonder if they should been notified?"

"I would be a little concerned about notifying them, Bob. I am sure they would want to know but would Eddie want them to? You know he must have considered it and might not want them to know about their mother just yet. You might want to discuss it with him but I suggest you don't push."

"I guess you are right, at least not while Gladys is in the condition she is in."

Changing to a happier subject, Bob asked, "Would you like to join me for dinner on Sunday? John and Sue Bolton wanted me to meet Mrs. Bolton."

"Oh, I'm sorry, but I'm going to be busy at church. What a shame. Sue Bolton - I think I have met her. Is she a very pretty tall blond?"

"I think so; I didn't really get a chance to look her over that well."

"Okay, Bob, who are you kidding, tell the truth here."

"Well, okay, yes she is a very pretty young lady."

"Ho-ho, and she might have her eyes on a certain young hero I know."

"Would you be jealous?"

"Maybe not exactly jealous, but concerned."

"I'm sure you don't have to be very concerned, I'm just going for dinner."

Bob and Ellen enjoyed a fine dinner and, after an after-dinner drink, they took a ride up to Enger Park, parked a while and viewed the city and harbor at night. It was evident they were beginning to enjoy each other's company more and more.

"Ellen, I have to tell you, I have not had any visions since talking to Father Tim O'Brian and being hypnotized by Dr. Fairchild. It is rather embarrassing to admit it was all necessary but my mind is much more at ease now. I seem to have lost the feeling of mental restraint that existed before. It feels like an unseen load has been lifted. I hope you don't feel like I am some sort of a mental case, but being with you has recently taken on an entirely new feeling. A feeling of trust, sort of a comfort I cannot quite explain but I feel I can confide in you without fear or need to hold back. I just want you to know how happy I am to have you as a friend."

"Thank you, Bob. I am happy to have you for a friend, too. And thank you for opening up to me; it means a lot to me."

She reached over and put an arm around Bob hugging him a little closer to her.

Visits To Gladys

"**G**OOD MORNING, MRS. LARSON. I am Father Tim O'Brian, how are you this morning?"

Gladys stared at him with a frightened look on her face and did not speak. Father Tim sat in a chair near the bed and continued talking. At first it was just idle talk, not directed at Gladys but storytelling to make her a little more comfortable with his presence.

"This has sure become an impressive hospital. I see all the fine furnishings in these pleasant rooms. There is the sunny exposure and lovely view on this side of the building. If one must be in the hospital, this is certainly a good place to be.

I remember the old one with its dark halls and bare rooms. My mother was here for an operation many years ago. I was quite young and not allowed to come to the rooms. She was here when my little brother was born. I really wanted to come in and see him so my Dad sneaked me in one evening after hours with the help of a friendly nurse we knew. I was just so tickled."

Father Tim noticed just a hint of a smile on Gladys' face, so he thought he would venture a question to see if he could get her to respond. Just then, a nurse brought in a tray in with some juice, fruit and coffee.

"Well now, that looks good. Do you like the food here?"

Gladys picked up an apple from the tray and threw it at Father Tim. He quickly reached up and caught it. He stood up and carefully placed it back on her tray and smiled. She looked him in the eye and smiled back.

"I have to go now, Gladys. Maybe I will stop in and see you again tomorrow. Bye."

She did not reply but watched as he walked out. Just outside the doorway he turned, smiled and waved to her. He could see a partially formed smile on her pale and haggard looking face.

Father Tim talked to his friend, Doctor Fairchild, relating the details of his visit with Gladys.

"Charles, I would appreciate if you would drop in on the lady and see what you feel can be done. She has experienced severe personal trauma and feelings of guilt for having cheated on her husband, causing the death of the man she slept with and causing her husband to suffer being shot in the leg. She seems to be in some kind of shock. Her response to my visit was minimal."

"Alright, Tim, I will pay her a visit although I suspect this could be a difficult case. Guilt can be a deep seated problem."

"I will appreciate whatever you can do."

⚔ Sunday Dinner ⚔

"COME IN; COME IN! Thank you for coming, Bob. My wife has been so anxious to meet you. --- Honey --- he is here!"

John Bolton's wife, Margaret, and daughter, Sue, welcomed Bob inside.

"Oh Bob, it's wonderful to meet you. I am so sorry I was unable to attend your award ceremony but I want to thank you for saving my John and Sue. I just cannot bear to think what could have happened if you had not been there."

"Well, Mrs. Bolton, we do what we have to do and no one is more thankful than I am for being there to help."

Sue joined in, "We're all so happy you could join us today."

"What a surprise you were, Sue, to find I was helping a pretty young lady instead of a guy off that locomotive. If I may be a little bold --- you clean up real nice."

"I like being with Dad on that locomotive so much. I'm happy to dress just like him when we are out there together --- but thanks for the compliment, I guess."

"Is it your plan to actually become a locomotive engineer as an occupation?"

"I guess it is a little unusual for a woman to want to become a locomotive engineer but I do like running that big engine. It's kind of a thrill to pull back on that throttle, hear that diesel bark and walk away down the track with a hundred cars of freight. Pulling the rope and blowing that whistle lets everybody know here I come, clear the way. But honestly, the answer to your question is, I don't know. I have also taken a course on semi-driving and that too is fun--- rolling down the highway with an eighteen wheeler and yakking on the CB radio while enjoying the countryside. Who knows, I'm sort of experimenting while I have the opportunity. I'll probably end up changing diapers for a flock of kids."

"Sounds like you are enjoying a full exciting life."

Margaret asked, "What about you Bob? I understand you are from the Twin Cities, what brought you to Duluth?"

"Actually it was a couple of fisherman." Bob gave them an abbreviated version of his education and need to check out new horizons.

"Interesting. See that, Margaret, good things happen to fishermen. I must get out and do more of it," said John.

"Do you work, Margaret?"

"Yes, I am a librarian at Jefferson school. I love being around the kids. I have been trying to encourage Sue to go into teaching but have not been too successful as you can see."

It was a very happy group who sat at the dining room table and enjoyed a great chicken dinner with all the trimmings and a few glasses of wine. Dinner was soon over and it was time for Bob to leave.

Margaret said, "Bob, it has been such a pleasure having you. I hope we can have you over again some time."

Sue added, "Soon!"

They all laughed and Bob bid farewell. It seemed like an open invitation for Bob to become better acquainted with Sue but as he left he realized he had become too attached to Ellen to become involved with someone else.

Dr. Fairchild Visits Gladys

WHEN DR. CHARLES FAIRCHILD called on Gladys he found her lying on her back in bed, staring at the ceiling and fussing with the buckle on her restraints.

"Good morning, Gladys. I am Charles Fairchild. Do you remember me? How are you today?"

She faced him with a rather wild look in her eyes but she did not respond.

"Is that strap bothering you, Gladys?"

She looked at the strap and yelled, "Yes, I don't like it."

"Gladys, if I remove the strap can we talk?"

"Yes, take it off."

"Let me see if I can find someone to remove it, I will be right back."

He went to the nurses' station to check on what medication Gladys was being given, how frequently and when she last received it. He asked a nurse to accompany him and returned. He closed the door and asked the nurse to remove the restraints. Gladys sat up, rubbed her wrist and grinned. He asked the nurse to take a seat.

"Does that feel better, Gladys?"

"Yes."

"Does your arm hurt?"

"Yes, when I am tied down."

"How do you feel now, Gladys?"

"Very sad and lonely."

"Why is that, Gladys?"

"I hurt my husband and I killed a man. I am so sorry I can't stand it."

Gladys broke down sobbing. Dr. Fairchild got up, handed her a tissue and put his arm around her. He held her tenderly until she stopped sobbing and dried her eyes.

"Gladys, I'm sorry you feel this way. Let's think about it. Was what happened really your fault?"

She replied tearfully, barely able to speak.

"Yes, it was my fault. I cheated on my husband and I am so sorry. I feel so guilty and so dirty. My husband is a fine man and I am so ashamed. I don't know why I did such a thing."

He spoke to her in a quiet comforting manner.

"How did it happen, Gladys?"

"Well, he had this new car and wanted to give me a ride so I went along and then one thing led to another and we went out to dinner and had quite a few drinks. He seemed so nice and all so when he took me home I invited him in for apple pie and he brought some more wine. Oh it is too horrible to think about it." She broke down again.

"Gladys, I am beginning to see the picture and I think it was more his fault than yours. I have been told he was very capable of charming ladies and perhaps you fell under his influence. I know this must be very hard for you to tell me these things. Would you like to lie back and rest a few minutes?"

"Yes, I am tired."

"Alright, perhaps I can help you rest better. I have this little red ball on this chain. You lie back and watch the ball closely as I swing it back and forth in front of you."

"Are you going to hypnotize me?"

"Is it alright with you if I do? Perhaps we can ease your pain."

"Will the nurse stay here too?"

"Yes, she will be right here with me."

"Alright, I will watch the ball."

He proceeded to hypnotize her. He talked to her gently in a very soothing manner trying to get her subconscious to eliminate or forget some of the horror and guilt she was remembering and experiencing. She grimaced, twisted and even yelled while under hypnosis. When she finally settled down, he awakened her. She seemed quite relaxed.

The nurse brought her a cup of tea and the three soon became engaged in light conversation. He thanked her for being a good patient and said he would drop in on her tomorrow.

Dr. Fairchild went to Eddie's room.

"Hello, Ed, I am Doctor Charles Fairchild. Father Tim O'Brian asked me to stop in and visit with Gladys. I came from Gladys' room just now. It seems obvious she loves you very deeply. Your wife has been having a very difficult time blaming herself for everything that has happened and for having hurt you so much. I understand the man was very persuasive. I am of the opinion she was impressed and perhaps a bit gullible and, human nature being what it is, he took advantage of her. Ed, I would like to have your perspective and I would like to ask how you feel about Gladys."

"Thanks for stopping, Doctor. As you can probably imagine this has been quite an ordeal for me. It is obvious it has been very difficult for Gladys as well. I have to say my first impulse was extreme anger. How could she do this to me? However, as I think about it now, my feelings have changed. Gladys has been a good wife and mother. To the best of my knowledge, she has never stepped out of line before even though I'm sure she has had plenty of opportunity. My job has had me away from home a lot and I am sure there were times she was lonesome or at least bored. I must admit this event does hurt but I do forgive her. I do love her very much. I want us both to heal and get this behind us as quickly as possible."

"Eddie, this sounds like a very good attitude. I understand you are due to leave the hospital tomorrow. Gladys is in a very fragile state of mind however if she fully understood your feelings she might be able to leave tomorrow as well. Would you like it if you could leave together?"

"That would be great."

"Let's go to her room together and see how she reacts in your presence. I am sure it will be awkward and difficult for both of you but if you can get over this hurdle and she can realize you are sincere in your forgiveness and your love for her, it will go a long way toward furthering her healing."

"OK, Doctor, I will try to be as convincing as possible and thanks for your help."

Eddie was able to walk now with the aid of crutches. He and the doctor made their way to Gladys' room. Eddie stood in the doorway with the doctor behind him. Eddie and Gladys looked at each other and neither said anything for a few moments. Then Eddie walked to her bed, sat on the edge and put an arm around Gladys. He hugged her and kissed her forehead. The doctor stood out of sight and listened.

"Oh, Eddie, I am so sorry, I have hurt you so much. I will never forgive myself."

"Gladys, I forgive you. I understand and I forgive you and I love you very much as I always have. We all make mistakes. You have been a wonderful wife and mother. I want to see you well again."

Gladys reached up and hugged him. Pulling him close to her, she kissed him.

"Eddie, I love you too. You have been so good to me all our lives. It pains me to no end to know I have hurt you so much."

"Gladys, I am being released from the hospital tomorrow. I will need these crutches for a short while but my leg is healing just fine. Would you like to leave with me so we can go home and get on with our lives?"

"Yes, Eddie. I know our flowers need tending, the birds need feeding, and oh there will be so much to do. We can do it together."

"Yes, Gladys, I will not go back to work for a while so we can spend a lot of time together. If you would like, I will ask my friend Bob to pick us up and we will go out to lunch together."

"Eddie, you are so thoughtful. I would like that."

Dr. Fairchild stepped into the room smiling.

"Well, it looks like you two are getting to know each other all over again. That is wonderful. I will leave you alone so you can spend the rest of the day together. You might even want to go to the cafeteria for lunch and then spend time in the sun room at the other end of the hospital. The view is nice from there."

Eddie said, "That sounds like a great idea. Thanks so much, Doctor." Dr. Fairchild left happily feeling that he had brought the couple together successfully.

Gladys and Eddie spent the rest of the day together happily renewing their love for each other and planning their future. Gladys lapsed into brief periods of uncertainty but Eddie comforted her as they shared the joy of being together again.

⚜ Leaving the Hospital ⚜

I T WAS ABOUT TEN o'clock in the morning when Bob arrived to pick up Eddie and Gladys. They signed all the necessary releases and were soon in Bob's car heading out to begin life anew. On their way home, Bob planned to take them to a popular restaurant on the waterfront.

It would be cool near the lake, so they decided to drive to the house first and pick up jackets. Bob helped Eddie out of the car and to the door. Eddie unlocked the door and went to the hall closet. Gladys went up the stairs to another closet for her jacket. She turned to head back down and saw the large blood stain on the floor at her feet. It was Eddie's blood. She looked down the hall and saw the large hole in the wall from the shotgun blast.

She ran back down the stairs to the front door screaming. "Oh my God I can't live here." She was screaming and crying as she ran out the door to Eddie and Bob.

Eddie grabbed her, put his arm around her and held her. "Don't cry, Gladys. Don't be afraid. We will clean everything up and it will be like new again."

"Oh, Eddie, how can I ever go into that bedroom again?"

"It is okay, Gladys. We will take care of everything. We will stay somewhere else until we get the place all cleaned up. I know it is hard for you, honey, but don't think about it now. Let's just go out for a nice lunch."

Bob said, "I have room at my apartment. You can both stay there until we get the work completed at your house. I will take you there after lunch and get someone started on the house immediately. I will get some of the boys from the office to help and we will have the place as good as new in no time."

Gladys said, "But the memories will still be there."

Eddie said, "Gladys, if it is still a problem after we fix up the house, we will sell it and buy a different one."

"Oh, God, what have I done?" wailed Gladys.

Eddie and Gladys got into the back seat of Bob's car and they drove to the lakefront. They found a table near a large window with a view of the water. Gladys settled down as they ordered a glass of wine and had a nice quiet lunch.

Bob remarked, "I'm going to have to bring Ellen here for dinner some evening. I think she'd really like it."

"Gladys and I used to come here quite a bit when we were younger. They sometimes had a small band and Gladys and I would dance with the best of them. By golly, Gladys, we are going to have to do that again just as soon as my leg is back in shape."

"Let's make it a double date. I'll ask Ellen and we will have a great time."

Eddie said, "Great! They used to have a great fish fry on Friday nights and prime rib on Saturdays and sometimes even the double bubble. Gladys and I sometimes even got a little tipsy on those nights."

Bob said, "I am buying, so let's have another wine in honor of the good old days at the lakefront."

Gladys responded quietly, "They weren't always good old days at the lakefront. My parents both drowned right out there near the lift bridge."

"Oh my God! I'm so sorry," said Bob looking at Eddie.

"Yes, it was a long time ago, but Gladys' parents were on a speed boat ride with friends of theirs. The driver wasn't watching carefully enough and collided with another boat coming under the bridge. The boat sank quickly in very deep water and they were never found. We were all devastated."

"How terrible."

"Yes, it was shortly after Gladys and I were married. It was so sad but in a way it brought us closer together. It was our love for each other that got us through that difficult time."

Eddie reached across the table and held Gladys' hand and said, "And it will be our love for each other that will bring us through this difficulty too."

Gladys looked at Eddie with tears in her eyes and didn't speak.

Eddie got up, put his arm around Gladys and kissed her forehead.

He reached around to a nearby chair for his crutches, turned to Bob and said, "Take us for a ride around the shoreline. Gladys always likes the view."

"Okay, let's do it."

They got up to leave with Bob leading the way, Gladys behind him and Eddie following on his crutches. Just after stepping out the door, Gladys turned, pushed Eddie aside and ran down the pier toward the water crying, "Mom! Mom!" as she ran.

Bob turned and ran after her but was unable to catch her. She ran as fast as she could. Gladys got to the end of the pier and jumped headlong into the lake. Everyone was astonished.

Bob yelled out, "Call 9-1-1" and jumped in after her. Bystanders ran inside and called for help.

Bob struggled to see beneath the murky water. He rose to the surface but could see no signs of currents moving. He dove again but could do nothing but grasp in the darkness. His lungs burned as he finally came up for air. Dejectedly, he pulled himself back onto the pier and cried.

A fire department rescue team arrived within minutes. They launched a boat and divers worked the rest of the day but were unable to find Gladys' body.

Eddie collapsed and was taken back to the hospital in shock. Bob stayed with him throughout the balance of the day. The grief was almost more than Eddie could handle. He was given sedation and finally went to sleep.

It was dark when Bob got home to his apartment. Bob called Ellen and shared the tragic events. She was flabbergasted.

"Oh my God! I cannot believe what has happened. This is so terrible. Are you OK? Poor Eddie. Is he going to make it?"

"He will certainly have a difficult time, but I am sure he will make it. He did everything he could to convince her he had forgiven her and that he loved her but she was just too fragile to deal with it. I feel so bad. I never should have taken them there."

"Oh, Bob, you had no way of knowing. You risked your own life to save her."

"I thought things were getting better, but none of us saw that she was just too fragile to deal with it."

"It is the saddest thing I ever heard of. How are you holding up?"

"I will be okay. I am going to have something to eat and then go back to the hospital and check in on him. Would you care to go along?"

"Of course. But mainly I want to see how you are doing."

Bob picked her up and they decided neither was very hungry, so they decided to go for pizza.

They arrived at the hospital to find Eddie awake. It was hard for him to keep from crying but he did manage to carry on a conversation.

"My Gladys is gone and I just cannot believe it. I should never have brought up the fact of her parents drowning. It was so long ago, I was sure that pain was over but it just added to her condition today. She was always so sensitive. I guess it was just more than she could handle."

"Eddie this entire event has been such a tragedy beyond belief. I know you are strong but I hope you are strong enough to handle all this pain and grief. Remember, my friend, I am here to help. Do not hesitate to ask if there is anything at all you need."

"Thanks, Bob, I really appreciate that. I just want to get out of here and then I will have to do something about a memorial service for Gladys."

Ellen spoke up, "Eddie if you can give me an idea what you would like, I will take care of it for you.

"Thank you, Ellen. Let me think about it tonight and we can talk tomorrow. As you are aware, throughout all of this I have not told anything to my daughters. Now I absolutely must give them the sad news. They both live in Los Angeles. It is going to be difficult to tell them but it has to be done." He broke down crying at the thought of telling them of their mother's death.

Ellen said, "Eddie, shall we do it together? Do you have the phone numbers with you? Perhaps we could call them from here right now."

"Yes, I have the numbers in my billfold. Here, I will get them out. The girls are Marsha and Sandy. They live quite near each other. We can call Marsha and she can tell her sister."

Bob used the room phone and dialed the number.

"Hello, this is Marsha."

"Hello Marsha, my name is Bob Nason. I am a friend of your father and am here with him at the hospital in Duluth. And Marsha, I'm sorry to say we have some very bad news. Your father is alright but at the moment is too grief-stricken to speak. Marsha, I'm calling because there has been an accident and your mother has passed away."

"Oh, no! Oh my God! Oh, no! ---- What happened?" Marsha broke down and cried. Bob waited for a few moments before he continued.

"Well, Marsha, I am so sorry for your loss."

Marsha gulped through tears as she spoke, "What happened? You said it was an accident? Was Dad hurt?" More tears followed. Bob waited patiently for the right time to speak.

"It is a very long story, but your mother drowned in Lake Superior. We will give you all the details when we see you. Your father hopes you can come here. We will be planning a memorial service soon."

"Poor Mom! I can't believe it! How is Dad?"

"Your father is heartbroken, of course. Here, I will let you talk to him."

Bob turned the phone over to Eddie.

"Hi honey. It is so sad, (crying). I loved her so much and now she is gone."

"Oh Dad, I know. Please hold on. I'll take the first flight out in the morning. I am so sorry, how are you?"

"I'll be okay. Will you tell Sandy?"

"Yes, I will tell her right away. We will both come as soon as possible. I love you, Dad."

"I love you, too, Marsha. Bye."

Ellen and her mother, along with Eddie and Father O'Brian planned a service for Gladys with a luncheon in the church hall. It was indeed a very sorrowful day for all who knew and loved her. After the details became known, some remarked about the irony of her going in the same way her parents had and in the same general location. When the memorial service was over and his daughters had gone back to California, Eddie was left to face his future alone.

⇥ Bachelors ⇤

B OB ARRANGED FOR EDDIE to stay with him until they could get Eddie's house back in shape. They installed new carpeting, had a carpenter repair the damaged wall and disposed of the bedroom furniture along with all of Gladys' belongings. Eddie had loved Gladys dearly but thought it was best to eliminate any reminders of the event with Marty.

As time went on, Eddie's physical and emotional wounds healed and even some of the scars disappeared. Eddie was walking well with just a little help of a cane and it wouldn't be long before he would not even need the cane and expected he would be able to return to work.

Ellen and her mother helped pick out new furniture and did some re-decorating. It wasn't long before everything was ready for Eddie to return home. He didn't want to go back alone, so Bob stayed with him for a few days, and then a few more days.

After a little while, they both decided that Bob should leave his apartment and move in with Eddie permanently. It wasn't long after, that Eddie was able to return to work so he and Bob were again together on the job.

Bob had not been home to visit with his parents for some time so after things had settled down, he left on a Saturday morning and drove home to New Brighton. His parents were happy to hear that he was doing well and had made new friends in Duluth. They were particularly interested in hearing about his friend, Ellen, saying they hoped he would bring her along to meet them soon. After visiting for a few hours, with his parents he had to head back. He promised that he would visit them more often in the future.

Bob left the house and drove to the cemetery. He walked in and looked at the headstones of his friends. He sat on the same stone bench where he had encountered visions. He sat there and watched the sun go down. He sat there and thought about Betty as twilight turned to darkness. The quiet of the evening settled over the cemetery as he sat there alone. He had recurring distant thoughts of Betty but there was no vision, no strong connection with the past. No ghost. He felt free. The past was behind him. He felt good as he walked out of the cemetery and headed back toward Duluth with thoughts of Ellen.

A few days later, he stopped in to see Dr. Fairchild. Bob explained that he had not experienced any visions since he had been hypnotized. He told Dr. Fairchild that he had tested the "cure" by going back to the cemetery. He explained that he had gone back and visited the cemetery where Betty was buried and was delighted to find that there was no recurrence. He told the doctor what a sense of freedom he felt when he left the cemetery.

He asked Dr. Fairchild if he could be confident that this was now a matter of the past and something he should not expect to be troubled about in the future.

"Well, young man, you are definitely over the hump. You experienced some horrible circumstances that made strong impressions on your psyche but, as they say, time heals all wounds. You will always remember your friend Betty but not in the same way. That was then and this is now. There is nothing you can do about the past and you should not dwell on it. Feel free to go forward and make a happy future for yourself. Rest assured that this is what Betty would want you to do."

⚞ Surprises ⚟

A S TIME WENT ON, Bob and Ellen grew closer and closer. Ellen and her mother were frequent companions of Bob and Eddie. They became a foursome, enjoying entertaining times together regularly. They were out for dinner on Friday evenings very frequently.

One Saturday morning while Bob was at the station buying gas he noticed a sign at the cash register. "Check your tickets - we are waiting for the winner: 7888-9722-10 55."

Bob had bought some tickets there a while back but really had not checked for the winning numbers. When he went home he searched the pockets of his jackets and found a number of tickets there. He routinely looked at the numbers, tossing many slips aside, until glancing at the final one. He was astounded. The numbers matched. The date matched. He had the winning ticket!!

After checking and double-checking, he reviewed the rules and found he would have almost a year before he would have to claim the winnings. According to the records, his ticket was worth $40 million! What would he do now? Bob had to think.

He put the ticket in his "fire safe" and drove up to the park. He sat there for a long while and thought about all that had happened to him since high school. He tried to remember what he wanted from life when it was simple and carefree. He looked at the stars and was grateful that he had been blessed with his family and friends – both present and past.

He decided he would not claim the winnings right away. He would tell no one about this until he could settle himself down and make a rational decision. He thought of the many things he could do with all that money. This was almost beyond his comprehension. He trusted that he would be shown the way.

As time went on, it was evident Ellen's mother and Eddie were becoming very close friends. Mary was well aware that Eddie had loved Gladys very much and there were times he still missed her, so she made no attempt to take Gladys' place. Mary was always gracious and friendly and, as time went on, Eddie became more fond of her.

Mary was an excellent cook and often came over and prepared some outstanding dishes for the four of them to enjoy. There were times when Mary and Eddie preferred to stay home together while Ellen and Bob went out for the evening.

After returning from the Twin Cities, Bob became less inhibited. He was more expressive and loving with Ellen. His arm was frequently around her. There were soon great hugs and kisses. It was obvious to all that they loved each other.

⊰ Sarah has News ⊱

O NE DAY BOB RECEIVED a letter from Sarah:

Dear Bob,

I cannot believe so much time has passed and so much as happened since you went away. There is so much I want to tell you. I am sure you remember Dr. Severson, your dentist who had his office over on Silver Lake Road. Anyway, his wife passed away last year with cancer. She was a sister of Johnny's mother Emily.

It is a long story but when my mother was down here visiting, she and Dr. Severson got acquainted. He hired Mom to work as a live-in maid at his big house right over near here on Long Lake. In a short while she was working at the house and also helping with the bookwork at his office. He and Mom fell in love and they were married in a small wedding last Saturday.

You might also remember the Severson's son, Clayton. He will soon be graduating from dental college and will be joining his father in the same office. He is such a nice man and we have become very close. We have not set a definite date yet, but wedding bells will be ringing here again.

I hope you will be able to attend the wedding. Little Johnny Jr. is growing like a weed and is such a joy to all of us.

I took a job teaching basic computer at the local vo-tech and love it. I hope you are well and happy. Be sure to stop in and visit when you next come to town.

The best to you always,
Sarah

That evening, Bob phoned Sarah. "I just received your letter today and just had to call. I am so delighted at all that has been happening. Sarah you deserve all the good things that are happening to you."

"I am happy you called, Bob. Do you remember the Seversons?"

"Sure I remember Doc well and Clayton, too. He was a good guy. He took Johnny and me out on Long Lake in his boat many times when we were younger."

"I am happy to hear you liked him Bob. He remembers you, too. He has been so nice to me and little Johnny and, of course, you know they are related. They are second cousins, and he and Johnny were good friends too."

"Well, Sarah, I couldn't be happier. Be sure to keep me informed so I can attend the wedding."

"I sure will. It is so nice to talk to you Bob, Bye"

"Bye Sarah."

One day, Bob stopped in at the Duluth Travel Agency and picked up some brochures. He brought them home and seemed to be studying them seriously. Eddie questioned him, "Are you really thinking about taking a trip, Bob, or just pipe dreaming?"

"Maybe a little of each, Eddie. Have you ever been on a cruise?"

"No, but I'm sure it would be fun to sail out on the ocean blue on one of those big ships"

"That's kind of what I have been thinking too. I saw some pictures in the window at the travel office and it kind of gave me the bug, I guess."

"Well, Bob, we will have to save up our nickels and maybe we can do it someday."

"Where do you think you would like to go, Ed?"

"Oh, I don't really know, never thought about it much. Let's ask the girls if they can think of some good places."

"Wouldn't that be great if we took the two them on a trip?

Bob said, "Well now, that is something to think about." Bob kept bringing home brochures and he and Ed kept thinking about the many wonderful places it would be possible to go. When the girls were over, the subject of travel came up frequently. Mary and Ellen were always excited by the thought of visiting faraway places but as they all realized, travels would be very expensive, so for now they would have to wait and save. Bob made no mention of his winnings.

One evening, Bob and Ellen returned from a movie to find Eddie and Mary sitting closer than usual on the sofa. They each had a drink in their hand. When Bob and Ellen walked into the living room, Eddie rose and motioned for them to sit on a nearby loveseat. He hurried to the kitchen and returned with two glasses of champagne.

He gave them each a glass and held his up saying, "Now, my young friends, Mary and I have an announcement to make. We have decided to get married. Let us all drink a toast to that!"

Ellen took a drink, set her glass down and ran to her mother. "Oh Mom, is this really true?"

"Yes, Ellen. We have been discussing it for some time now. I know Eddie is a fine man and I have fallen in love with him. Your father has been gone a long time now and I know he would approve."

"Mom, I am so happy for you. And you, too, Eddie," She ran over to him and gave him a big hug.

Bob shook Ed's hand and hugged him.

"Congratulations, old friend, I couldn't be happier. Actually, I am not surprised. You two seemed to hit it off right from the beginning." He gave Mary a big hug too.

"Eddie, I will take a re-fill. This calls for more champagne," said Bob.

They were a very happy group as they celebrated the occasion that night.

Bob and Ellen began spending more and more time together as Eddie and Mary were busy getting started on wedding plans. It was evident that they, too, had fallen in love.

One evening, Bob and Ellen drove out to the Hideout and had dinner in one of the private cubicles. They loved being together. They always had interesting private conversations. After a delicious dinner and a couple of drinks, and while waiting for the soufflé to arrive, Bob reached into his inside coat pocket and brought out a small box. He opened it in front of Ellen, displaying a beautiful diamond ring. She opened her mouth and gasped.

Bob reached across the table, placing his right hand on hers and said, "Ellen, I love you. Will you marry me?"

With tears in her eyes she said, "Oh Bob, I love you so much. Yes, yes. I will be happy to marry you!"

He reached across and slipped the ring on her finger, then leaned over the table and kissed her sweetly.

Tears welled in her eyes as she looked at the ring and said, "Bob, I have loved you since the day we met."

Bob said, "I have loved you for a long time, too."

As they realized the plans that would need to follow, Bob asked Ellen, "What would you think of the idea of making it a double ceremony with your Mom and Eddie?"

Without hesitation, Ellen replied, "I think that would be great."

When Bob and Ellen arrived at Eddie's house, he and Mary were discussing plans for their own wedding. Bob and Ellen went to the kitchen and returned with a bottle of champagne and four glasses. With a deliberate swag, Bob placed the bottle and glasses on the table as Ellen held out her hand to display the new diamond ring.

Eddie looked up and said, "Is this what I think it means?"

"Indeed it is, so let's have a toast to my bride-to-be."

Mary jumped up and hugged both Ellen and Bob.

"This is wonderful news, let's have a double ceremony!"

"And let's go on a honeymoon together," said Eddie excitedly.

And so it was. That weekend, the four drove to New Brighton to inform Bob's parents of the good news. Ellen and Mary worked on the planning together. They selected a date and arranged for Father Tim O'Brian to perform the ceremony.

When it was time to decide on a honeymoon trip, Eddie and Mary added up what they had in savings. Ellen did too. It was evident their combined funds would not permit a long trip but they were all happy as long as they could be together.

The next day, Bob went down to the station with his winning lottery ticket. He took the manager aside and requested that he be as quiet and confidential as possible and the two made arrangements with the lottery commission for the payoff.

Bob was immediately a very rich man. With the knowledge he would be getting an enormous amount of money, he formulated a plan for preserving it. He deposited one million in one bank which could be used at any time. The balance was distributed in accounts at several banks and in U.S. Treasury notes.

That night, Bob told Ellen, Mary and Eddie that he needed to have a serious discussion with them. They convened at the dining room table, somewhat nervous about the tone of Bob's request. Sitting at the head of the table, Bob took out a pad of paper and pen.

"I need to tell you something that will cause some major changes in each of our lives. It may be difficult to accept, but I believe that our love and friendship will see us through this adjustment."

Ellen reached for Bob's hand. "What is it, honey? You're scaring me."

Eddie blurted out, "Geez, Bob, whatever it is, we'll figure out a way to get through it."

Mary nodded solemnly with tears in her eyes.

Bob lifted his pen and wrote on the pad. He tore off the sheet and held it up for all to see. It read: $40,000,000.

Ellen shook her head and said, "Honey, I don't understand. Are you being sued?"

Bob wrote again, this time more slowly. All eyes were glued on him. He set his pen down, creased the paper and tore it off carefully.

Eddie piped up, "Just spit it out, Bob. You're killing me."

Bob held up the second sheet. It read: I WON THE LOTTERY!!!

Ellen screamed and jumped into Bob's arms. Mary grabbed Eddie around the neck, hugging him with all her might. Eddie choked out "Oh my God! Oh my God! Am I dreaming?"

After the tears and laughter had subsided, Bob spread travel brochures all across the table. He told the group that he had known about his winnings for some time but wanted to choose the right moment to celebrate his good fortune with them.

Ellen, Mary and Eddie were astonished beyond belief. As they sat down at the dining room table that evening Bob explained they could now travel anywhere they wished.

Eddie asked, "What are you saying Bob, you are a millionaire many times over?"

"Yes, Eddie, I have known I won the lottery for some time now, but I still cannot believe it."

Ellen said, "I don't know if I will be able to handle it. I don't know how to be the wife of a millionaire."

Bob said, "You will just have to be your wonderful self and we will all have to learn together."

Mary said, "I am on cloud nine and feeling giddy. I still can't believe what I am hearing."

Their surprise, elation and joy were beyond description as they settled down enough to plan the wedding and honeymoon. The size of the guest list was increased and the wedding reception was made more elaborate. Money was no longer an object.

Immediately after the wedding, the newlyweds, Bob's parents and Eddie's daughters left to see the world.

The last anyone heard, they were somewhere in the south of France.

Other books by Clifford C. Leary are:

Grandpa Cliff Remembers
Grandpa Cliff's Verses
Grandpa Cliff's Tales

⚔ About the Author ⚔

THE AUTHOR IS AN 84 year old retired railroad vice president. He was raised on a dairy farm, graduated from high school at 17 and went into concrete silo construction. At the end of the construction season he went to work as a station helper and worked his way up to vice president of transportation. After retiring at age 55 he went into real-estate. He remodeled and rented several homes and started writing as a hobby. He has written three books which are available on Amazon and Barnes and Noble. "Grandpa Cliff Remembers", "Grandpa Cliff's Tales", and "Grandpa Cliff's Verses".